In **Part 1**, Cyril Fother⟨...⟩ W9-APL-919 could destroy the world ⟨...⟩ ⟨...⟩ British prime minister, Cyril and his trusted cohort, Geoffrey Cowlishaw, travel to Italy. . .to a top-secret meeting with Pope Adolfo I. On the way, Cyril and Geoffrey make some amazing discoveries and witness a dramatic self-sacrifice.

In **Part 2**, Cyril and Geoffrey discover the greatest obstacle to their top-secret mission: Baldasarre Gervasio, the pope's most trusted advisor, reviled as the "ratman." After Cyril discovers Gervasio's secret "experiments," he is followed into Gervasio's underground kingdom—the Roman catacombs—by a horde of trained rats who wait only for their master's command.

In **Part 3**, after a miraculous escape from the catacombs, Cyril begins his journey home to England, accompanied by Henry Letchworth. Signs of a sinister betrayal abound as the two men are shipwrecked and encounter a group of Druids bent on their destruction.

Now, Roger Elwood's
riveting six-part adventure
continues with. . .

PART 4
THE JUDAS FACTOR

Roger Elwood, whose gripping suspense titles have occupied best-seller lists over the past ten years, is well known to readers of Christian fiction. Such Elwood page-turners as *Angelwalk*, *Fallen Angel*, *Stedfast*, and *Darien* have together sold more than 400,000 copies.

A RIVETING SIX-PART ADVENTURE

PART 4
WITHOUT THE DAWN

THE JUDAS FACTOR

ROGER
ELWOOD

BARBOUR
PUBLISHING, INC.
Uhrichsville, Ohio

© MCMXCVII by Roger Elwood

ISBN 1-57748-041-4

Published by Barbour Publishing, Inc.
P.O. Box 719
Uhrichsville, Ohio 44683
http://www.barbourbooks.com

 Member of the
Evangelical Christian
Publishers Association

Printed in the United States of America.

CHAPTER 1

Neither Cyril nor Henry actually lost consciousness, though they came close.

Both were dazed when they hit a moss-covered section of rock floor finally, pain traveling through their bodies. No bones were broken by the impact, though wrenched, strained muscles protested as the two men tried to stand, wobbled, then fell back.

Resting briefly, they glanced at their surroundings.

A cavern.

It would have been absolutely dark if not for several holes in the ceiling, which channeled the faintest strands of moonlight, giving luminance.

And candles.

The cavern was ringed with scores of long candles, not yet melted down to half their original size.

"They were going to come back here," Cyril speculated, "and continue with their ceremonies. From what I heard a number of years ago, Druids have rites for every purpose, and not all of these are of malevolent intent."

Some were designed to appeal to their gods for rain. Others covered rodent attacks and crows as well as locust infestations and similar problems long associated with a rural lifestyle. But at the core of the Druid practices was extreme violence, the taking of life, born or unborn, all of it done within an occultic framework.

"This might be where the Druid remnant had been conducting their ceremonies for hundreds of years," Cyril said as he managed to stay on his feet without falling again.

Henry mumbled a reply while walking toward an elevated section of rock that looked much like a podium in a cathedral.

"Do you feel it?" he asked as he climbed on top.

Cyril had to confess that he did.

Iniquity.

Not simply isolated acts of sin performed in dark places, or a rockbound underground love nest frequented by young men and their conquests.

Far worse.

The essence of all sin, a direct link with the evil one, Satan.

"It would not be difficult to imagine that this is where evil originated," Henry went on. "I know that is not true, but then the alternative must be that so much evil has occurred here unabated that the very air seems filled with it."

The air. . . .

Very much like what they had detected in the woods, dry and lifeless.

"Men and women who by their very nature cause the angels to weep. . ." Cyril mused.

Henry was moved.

"I have not heard that before, my brother," he remarked. "Did you read it somewhere or is it entirely yours?"

"It is mine."

Henry bowed his head but did not close his eyes. He was not praying but looking into himself, trying to focus his mind on where they were and why.

"The Druids are far more evil than I ever knew," he admitted. "I once thought of them as rather harmless folks who should be left alone to live as they saw fit. How could they hurt anyone else? As long as their way of life did not affect mine, what was there to be concerned about?

"The ones we saw on the surface are surely dead, if those two so-called knights were as thorough as I suspect, but do any others remain, Cyril? Will we have to defend ourselves against them? How do we make contact with Lofton and Mottershead? They must be frantic, wondering where we are. So many questions but I cannot think of a single answer."

Abruptly, after cocking his head and sniffing the air, Henry jumped off the elevated section.

"Do you smell that?" he asked.

Cyril did but he could not identify the source.

"Like something—" he began.

"Dead," Henry suggested, "like something dead but not buried."

Cyril pointed in the direction of what appeared to be a tunnel connected to the cavern at the eastern end.

He started toward it.

"Let me go with you," Henry said. "We should not allow ourselves to become separated under any circumstances."

They walked slowly in that direction, hoping not to trip over anything unseen in their path, the candles and the feeble moonlight providing hardly sufficient light.

As they approached the natural archway that led into the tunnel, the odor became stronger.

"I wonder if I want to find out what is causing it," Henry said honestly, again echoing how Cyril felt as well.

A short tunnel.

Less than a dozen feet in length. Leading into another cavern considerably smaller than the one they had just left, a cavern that was being used as a makeshift storage area. The two men recoiled at the sight inside.

Babies.

At least a score of bodies, mostly skeletons but a few with some flesh still on them, and of these, two that could have been killed as recently as days before.

"The rejected ones," Cyril muttered, realizing in a flash why they were there.

"How do you know?" Henry asked.

"Study them, my friend, study the shape of their heads."

Henry saw that the babies were abnormal.

"Misshapen," he said, examining the bodies. "Some with very large foreheads, one with no eyes since the cavities in his skull where these would have been never developed properly, another with his nose and mouth all twisted up together."

"Precisely, Henry. I doubt that the Druids wanted to give imperfect sacrifices to their gods for fear that punishment would be meted out. These are children who would have grown up handicapped, unable to speak properly, unable to survive on their own by feeding themselves and taking care of other basic needs, unable to see or to hear.

"Still, many parents would have taken them and loved them and made life as pleasant as possible, but not the Druids. Trouble is, I know men and women who are *not* Druids yet they feel the same way. If a baby falls short of perfection, get rid of it.

"And remember, my brother, what you and I have learned. Druids believe in soul transference. That there is a possibility that these deformities will be perpetuated in *another* body, surely a *bête noire*—a thing to be feared—to them."

Henry returned his attention to the rejected babies.

"Would life for them have been so terrible?" he asked plaintively. "If only loving parents had gotten hold of such little ones."

Henry sat down on the hard stone floor and picked up one of the two tiny bodies that was not yet into any advanced state of deterioration, holding it in his arms.

"Here I might have been, Cyril, here I might have been but for the sweet grace of our blessed Heavenly Father," he said, looking up as moisture slipped from his eyes and streamed down both cheeks.

They hoped they could remember the location of that particular cavern because they wanted to make sure the bodies of those babies were removed later and buried properly.

"Like so much garbage," Henry muttered as they walked away. "How can anyone treat *life* in that way and yet not be assaulted by his conscience?"

"If the Druids are as corrupt as I now believe," Cyril suggested, "then it is likely that they no longer have a conscience as such."

Henry found that thought unnerving.

"Satan has his way with them?" he posed. "Is that what we might have to face, people utterly controlled by the devil?"

"I think, in some respects, that the Druids could be worse

than the Muslims. Frankly, not all Muslims are fanatical. They may be hopelessly duped by a heathen belief system but the majority seem peaceful enough, with no desire for vengeance. That is why I am unable to believe that *all* would approve of any plan for an epidemic, if they knew about it.

"But it is a different story with the Druids. They are not a race into which someone is born but a secret society that people of a like mind join. And if they had even the remnants of a conscience, they would not be instigators of such calamity in the first place."

"Is it not interesting, Henry," suggested Cyril, "that they are on the rise again during a period of time that has seen more cultic activities than virtually any other? I am thinking, of course, of Jonestown but also the Heaven's Gate group. They seemed nonviolent, in a sense, killing themselves, yes, but not taking with them any who did not want to be involved in the pact. The Druids are just as fanatical but their main objective is to save themselves while they murder others."

The two of them had been walking as they conversed.

"Hear that?" Henry asked abruptly.

Cyril stopped, trying to hear anything at all in that dismal underground maze.

Sobbing. . . .

"I think it is a woman," Henry said. "No, wait."

Others. Not just the first one.

"Several women. Near, Cyril, near."

They tried to check out the direction of the sounds.

"They seem so scared," Henry remarked.

"How can you tell? Their sobs might mean sorrow alone. I hear no screaming, no cries for help."

"By the trembling."

Cyril listened again carefully, out of respect for Henry, the sounds pitiful, admittedly, but he could attribute little else to them.

"Trembling?" he asked. "They cry, Henry, they do that for certain. But—"

"This is different," Henry interrupted. "Once on my

brother's ship we took some women from Scotland on down to Gibraltar."

"Quite a journey."

"It was. The women were frightened much of the way."

"And you learned to tell the difference between their crying, either from sadness or fear or whatever?"

"Yes, that is right, Cyril."

And he would do what he could to comfort them.

Sometimes Henry wondered whether their fear stemmed entirely from the rigors of the journey, buffeted as the ship was from extremes of weather, one day the sea calm, more like a huge lake in fact, the sun sending temperatures very high, the air oppressively humid, and then two days later, a sudden storm would arise so violent that it seemed the lives of *everyone* on board could not possibly be saved except by a direct intervention from God Himself; or whether their nervous condition came in part from what they would face when they reached their destination, a nation in Africa where many foreigners had settled, Europeans mostly, who, having forsaken the local prostitutes, still craved companionship and had purchased the women to be their wives.

"We should call out to them, tell them we mean no harm" Cyril said.

"They would become quiet then," Henry replied, "and we might pass near them without ever knowing that we had done so, which would be a pity."

"Why? We speak the same language. They would understand us."

"Yes, they would, but they might also think that we are Druids trying to trick them by disguising our intentions."

Smiling at his friend's astuteness, Cyril could not disagree.

"We should hope that they continue crying for just a little while longer," he said, dreading the reason for their fear.

They did just that, wherever they were, sometimes with enough hysteria that they ended up sounding more like the women of a Greek tragedy, weeping and wailing and hitting the ground with fists that soon would be bloodied.

It was all Cyril and Henry needed to find the women, which they did minutes later.

Both stood in front of the smallest cavern they had seen thus far.

They faced eight obviously pregnant, desperately frightened women, all hope drained from their pale faces. Those who were more aware of what was going on screamed as Cyril and Henry quietly entered the cavern.

"No!" they cried out, backing away, their eyes wide, expressions of terror stark on their careworn faces.

"You must not do this to us!" one of the women yelled.

It was Henry who stepped forward first.

"We are here to release you," he said. "Lord Fothergill and I are Christians, not satanists. You have nothing to fear, you and your babies."

The youngest of the women stopped screaming but turned away.

"Fothergill?" one of the women repeated.

Suddenly, instead of crying, they started to laugh, and laugh uproariously, all except the woman who had avoided their gaze. Cyril stepped beside Henry and introduced himself.

"Praise God!" they exclaimed together, managing to stand but uncertainly.

The remaining woman stayed where she was, not yet convinced that the lot of them were out of danger.

"What is wrong with her?" Cyril asked, more concerned than offended.

"Please talk to her, Lord Fothergill," one of the others said knowingly. "You will find out soon enough."

Cyril sat beside beside the woman but did not speak. He wanted her to become comfortable with his presence.

"You and the others seem to recognize my name," he said softly a few minutes later, while Henry sat among a gathering of the other women, and charmed them all, his occasional "vagueness" rather appealing to them.

At first the woman pointedly did not answer Cyril but

hugged herself.

"We will not do anything but take you and your companions to safety, leaving this awful place far behind."

He lowered his voice until it was hardly more than a whisper.

"Will you please trust my friend and I to do that?"

She relaxed her arms and finally looked up at him.

"You are not the first lord to be here," she said at last.

Cyril was not prepared for that.

"The Druids captured someone else?" he asked dumbly, raising his voice unintentionally and acting as though the woman were trying to deceive him.

She started to inch away, and became frantic when she bumped up against the rock wall of the cavern, acting like some trapped animal.

"You have nothing to fear from me or my friend Henry," Cyril told her. "Please. . .tell me. . .about the other lord."

Her eyes widened and he could see rank panic in them.

"Can you do that, madam? Can you tell me where would the Druids be keeping him? We must try to get the man to safety along with you and the other women here."

She shook her head.

"You do not know?" he asked.

She seemed to want to trust him but she had endured so much pain and terror that any stranger seemed a threat.

Cyril bowed his head and Henry followed his lead.

" 'What time I am afraid,' " he prayed from Psalm 56, " 'I will trust in thee. In God I will praise his word, in God I have put my trust; I will not fear what flesh can do unto me.' "

The women started weeping again but not for the same reason, quietly this time.

"We have prayed so much," one said. "We have prayed for the good Lord to send help, to get us out of this hellish place."

As Cyril was opening his eyes, he could feel the hesitant touch of someone's hand on his right shoulder.

"Forgive me," the woman said, "please forgive me,

dear sir."

"About the lord you mentioned," he continued, "after he was captured, do you know where they put him?"

"Not captured, sir," she corrected him, "this lord, I say, was one of them."

"Surely you are mistaken," he countered. "I cannot imagine—"

"The other lord was so evil," she interrupted, her apprehension intensifying. "He fooled all of us. At the beginning this one seemed righteous, kind, decent. His voice was so soothing, his features pleasing. But then we knew what he intended. He wanted our babies."

She became pale at the persistent thought of having her child taken from her grasp by brutal strangers.

"We were sure at first that you were his henchmen coming back to take the little ones to him."

Cyril was finding much of what the woman was telling him hard to accept since it seemed so relentlessly cruel.

"They are yet to be born, perhaps two or three months from now. How could even the Druids possibly stoop to this? I begin to ask myself if you are telling me the truth."

"I do not lie about such things, Lord Fothergill."

"And a man of nobility is involved, you say? Someone whose refinement was supposed to civilize him, separate him from the barbarians?"

She nodded, pointing toward the entrance to that little cavern.

"You missed him by just a few minutes."

"He was about to order our babies to be cut from us," another woman added, "when he was warned that some make-believe knights had stopped the sacrifice, and—"

"Do you know where the exit out of this maze is?" Cyril asked, excited.

"I think we can help you find it."

He was about to stand when he decided to ask her one another question: "Why did my family name seem so familiar, causing you to react as you did?"

She blushed and turned her head so that he would not see her expression. "Please, do not make me tell you, sir. Forgive me for ever mentioning anything."

Cyril did not want to appear that he was intimidating her but he also needed to know why his name should provoke such a reaction.

"How is it possible, madam?" he asked. "I am unable to say that we have ever met. I wish you would tell me."

Tears were streaking down her dirt-smudged cheeks.

"Must I, sir, must I really do that?" she asked.

"I know that you have been forced to do too much already and I will not insist. But I would be very grateful, now or later, if you would give me some idea."

She was trying to get up sufficient courage to tell him what he wanted to know.

"Because of Raymond, sir," she finally said, "because of Raymond Fothergill."

His father!

Cyril nearly fell on his back at the mention of a name that, in the final hours of the man's life, had become more important than ever before.

"But what do you know of my father?"

She hesitated again, more reluctant than ever.

"This is difficult, Lord Fothergill."

"First, tell me your name," he asked, trying to get her to relax.

"Fiona, sir."

"What is your last name?"

"The name of my father becomes the same as mine, yes?"

"That it does."

"Then my name is Fiona. . .Fiona Fothergill."

Cyril had been about to swallow as she spoke. What the woman told him made him start choking so badly that Henry had to come to his aid.

After he had recovered, he asked, "But how can you be sure? How can I know that you are telling the truth?"

"A woman who has been rescued from death at the

hands of men capable of the greatest evil does not lie to one who is her benefactor. My son will not now be cut from his mother's womb because of what you have saved us from.

"Can you believe me to be someone who would ever tell you something so false, so deceitful as the name of my father if it were not true? I may not be your social equal, Lord Fothergill, but I do hold some things in life sacred."

. . .cut from his mother's womb.

"Are you absolutely certain?" Cyril asked.

"*Yes!*" she cried. "I saw the knife. They did not have to *tell* me by any words from their dirty mouths. I knew what it was for!"

"They would not simply wait until the baby is born? And *then* sacrifice him?"

"No, if babies are not born in time for their ceremonies, those monsters cut open our stomachs and take the little ones. Few are allowed to come to full term, sir."

"And then the Druids would have just left you here to die?"

Overhearing what was being said, the other women murmured in agreement.

"Mothers have been known to bleed to death after the grisly business was done," one of them said, "and if not that, they starve, or cut their own throats to end the nightmare."

. . .my name is. . .Fiona Fothergill.

Cyril was shaken first by learning that his father, in his days of promiscuity, had actually fathered a daughter, and then, by what else he was now learning.

He glanced at each one of the women, seeing the telltale signs of their trade, the makeup now smeared all over their faces, the tawdry clothes, the hardness of their features.

"Are you all, eh—?" he started to ask but faltered.

Henry came to the rescue.

"What my friend wants to know is whether you all are plying a certain trade that calls for you to. . .to—?" he began, and then he, too, stumbled.

The women broke out in coarse laughter.

"Are we all prostitutes?" Fiona offered. "I must say that we are, sir. Abandoned by the men in our lives, we have had to make our way as best we could. None of us is proud of how we have spent the years since we were no longer virgins but our bodies were all we had, with no other skills to sustain us. If all else failed, we always had our babies."

"You gave up your children?" Cyril asked.

"Yes, good sir, but only to couples barren of fruit. Was that so wrong, I ask? Was that not wiser, kinder, more loving than having them die in an alley along with their mothers, for that is where most of our kind end up, you know, either that or on some Druid altar?"

"Or coughing our lungs out because of the cold, the rain, and no dry warm place to sleep," another added.

Raymond Fothergill was so desperate that he would reach out for the nearest prostitute and spend time with her rather than return to his own family.

And we drove him to it, Cyril thought. *We cut him off because of the way he was living, and he had nowhere else to turn.*

He brushed one finger against Fiona's cheek.

"How old are you?" he asked, thinking of Clarice and Sarah, and wondering what their lives would be like a few years later.

"Nineteen, Lord Fothergill."

Nineteen, he repeated to himself. *And you have probably been on the streets for two or three years at least, bedding down with anyone who would pay.*

"My father, he just abandoned you?" he asked, not quite prepared to believe that Raymond Fothergill had stooped to that level.

She bowed her head, not directly answering him.

"He was very lonely, sir," she said, unable to face him. "He went from woman to woman, I think, searching, hoping. . ."

"But we. . .we were always there, my family and I, *his* family, ready to help if he should ever need us."

He cringed a bit as he said that, knowing that it bordered on being a lie.

"But Raymond told me that he could never go back," Fiona replied.

Cyril wanted to rebut that but he could not.

"He knew you disapproved of the way he lived. He thought he would be under your scrutiny every minute he spent with you."

"Of course I disapproved, but not I alone, the rest of the family did as well. The man was drinking himself to death, and carousing from bed to bed."

"Do you ever have anything to do with Prime Minister Edling?" she asked.

He sensed that she was ready to spring some sort of trap but he felt unable to prevent this, given the direction of their conversation.

"Yes, I do," he acknowledged. "There are matters of business between us that must be dealt with from time to time."

Fiona's eyes narrowed as she stared at him.

"And you see nothing wrong in that?" she asked.

"Of course not. He is the highest elected official of my country. If I ignored him, if I pretended that he were of no consequence, he has the power to compel me to obey him."

"And your father does not? Is that why you turned away from him, breaking his heart?"

Cyril tried to keep his rising anger from getting out of hand.

"I have slept with Edling as well, Lord Fothergill," Fiona added. "Surely you have known that he does not lead a chaste life."

"I was not ignorant of his caprices but, after all, I can hardly avoid contact with the prime minister. If he summons me, I must go, whatever I think of his immoral personal life."

"But you treat your father as unnecessary then? You can ignore his pleas and turn your back on him so easily?"

Cyril was struggling to give her an answer that was completely honest.

"As a Christian, how could I tolerate any of that, Fiona? How could I do anything but reject the sin? I tried to be generous, to be understanding, but my father kept on doing what was contrary to so much that I hold sacred."

"Including consorting with prostitutes?" Fiona asked.

"Yes, including that," Cyril told her.

"Am I such a sinner then, sir, that vile men were about to do with me what they want, and it is all right?"

Her eyes were bulging with anger.

"Including ripping my baby from my womb?"

"Of course not, Fiona! Any man who believes that is making a travesty of his so-called faith. He borders on blasphemy."

"But you feel that my mother and her mother before that and myself, we all are sinners because we have done what the Bible forbids?"

"I have to say that that would be my conviction."

"What about forgiveness? What about the whole purpose of the Lord Jesus' death, burial, and Resurrection?"

"Are you suggesting that forgiveness is unlimited?"

Fiona nodded emphatically.

"It is what I have been taught by the priests, though some of *them* were more interested in my body than my soul."

"I regret that more than you know," Cyril told her, "and have complained louder than most that Adolfo should clean the church of its own corruption so that it can be a more worthy witness to an unregenerate world."

"So forgiveness is unlimited then?" she persisted.

"Well, I have to say that you and the priests are right," he commented, "but there is something you and they overlook."

"And what is that, Lord Fothergill?" she asked with a trace of sarcasm.

The other women, and Henry as well, were fascinated by the exchange.

"When Christ spoke to the woman who was caught in adultery, he told her, 'Go. . .and sin no more.' Her freedom to leave without being stoned to death by a mob was coupled with the absolute necessity to avoid any more adulterous relationships. None of us can keep sinning because we assume that grace is endless and will continue to abound whatever it is that we care to do with our lives."

"But if I will not lose my salvation—"

Cyril interrupted her.

"That much you do have right, Fiona. But God cannot look long at sin in *anyone's* life and then blithely turn away, as though it does not matter. He will punish, not by sending you to hell, but in other ways."

He paused to emphasize what he said next.

"Such as allowing you to be here now. You almost lost your baby in the most gruesome and painful manner. Can you not see that as a warning?"

"But you are here now, and it is not going to happen."

"What about the next time, Fiona? What about the diseases your way of life can bring upon you? What about the shameful things men force you to do? Is that the heritage you want to leave with your son or daughter?"

Fiona said nothing for a brief while, embarrassed at being with her father's son for the first time, and at having to tell him of moments so private she had never been able to reveal them to anyone else.

"Forgive me if I speak improperly, sir, but did Christ cast sinners from His presence or did He minister to them and try to get them to change their lives? How often did you or anyone else in the Fothergill family try to change your father's life, to get him to give up his sin?" She spoke candidly as she looked up at him. "Or did you just turn your back on him and leave it all in the hands of our Heavenly Father?"

"I never wanted to seem that I was soft toward his debauchery," he cried. "I never wanted to appear that I was excusing *any* of the sin in which he was engaged; I never wanted to give the impression that all Raymond Fothergill had to do was just return home and everything would be forgiven, and forgotten as well."

She took his hand and rested her palm on his own.

"But sir, is that not what the Lord Jesus Christ taught

when He described the prodigal son?"

"Until the last, my father never seemed eager to be free of the life he had been leading long before I got to know him. It was as though he were saying, 'This is the way I am. You and the Lord will just have to accept me.' I thought that his sin held him so tightly in its grip that he might never pull himself free of it."

Fiona Fothergill's voice became softer, losing what had been a hard edge.

"When did you give him a chance, Lord Fothergill, when did you do that?"

One of the women screamed abruptly. All swung to face the five hooded figures standing in the entrance to that alcove.

Each man was holding a .357 Magnum pistol.

CHAPTER 2

Elizabeth Fothergill was standing behind one of the family castle's parapets, looking out over their land, and studying the direction generally taken by Cyril Fothergill when he came home after one of his business trips.

No movement, human or otherwise.

Cyril had been away in the past for many weeks at a time, but never had she felt such unease over his absence.

Have you been swallowed up and I shall never see you again, despite my prayers on these poor knees of mine? she thought.

Elizabeth's knees had only recently begun to hurt. But since she was hardier of temperament and constitution than most wives of wealthy families, she tended to disregard any and all pain, shoving it out of her mind as though it did not exist, never letting anything of the sort stop her from living as she always had.

Cyril will see me walk with this slight limp and he will be desperately worried, thinking, before I can tell him the right of it, that I have injured myself in his absence. I wish I could send him a letter, perhaps care of Pope Adolfo. . . .

Many prayers had been offered by Elizabeth and most members of the Fothergill household staff, especially the security guards, men who felt the strongest rapport with Cyril, who considered him a man of dignity, courage, and decency.

Roger Prindiville was the most concerned of any of them.

"Lord Fothergill is so fine a man," he told Elizabeth as he stood beside her that afternoon, his own eyes searching the land. "I cannot see why the Savior would allow anything to happen to him."

"We do not know the mind of Almighty God," she said.

"There may be a reason for my husband never again to set foot in this home."

She did not mean this in any way to reflect upon the marital fidelity that kept them bonded to one another but Prindiville took her remark the wrong way and became tense, his muscles tightening, a dryness in his throat.

"But that would mean leaving behind those he loves, and those who love him," he commented sadly.

She corrected him with a sharp look that was not customary, but when she found it necessary, carried precisely the message that was meant. Then Elizabeth smiled, taking some of the edge off her rebuke.

"You speak like one who does," she observed.

Prindiville, embarrassed already, felt even more so now that she had been able to see through him so easily.

"I do, milady, I do. In my view, Lord Fothergill has a soul that seems as close to purity itself as I have seen in this blighted old world. And. . .and. . .I can scarce imagine how it would be. . .this life we lead. . .without him."

Elizabeth was pleased that he thought of Cyril in this way, but as much as she loved her husband, she knew that sinless perfection was not one of his encompassing virtues.

"But my husband is a sinner," she insisted, "as are the rest of us, you and me included, Mr. Prindiville. He is not so pure as you think."

"But there is so great a contrast between him and his father," he added, unconvinced.

Elizabeth had to agree with that.

"You are right, dear man, but let it be said that Raymond Fothergill is in heaven even as we speak, and he is there *despite* his conduct."

"So much to be washed clean," Prindiville mused.

"My husband certainly has a temper. He is moody. There exists in him a selfish streak. Furthermore, I am sure that he has told his share of lies. And in his youth he must have been bent on giving his father a run for the money. After all, what other example of masculine conduct could have more profoundly affected him?"

Elizabeth paused, thinking of something that seemed quite fresh to her.

"I had my time with him, you know," she said.

Prindiville looked disbelievingly at her.

"Oh, but I did. His randy ways were fading, mind you, and while he has never been unfaithful, nor have I, for that matter, still, the temptations came."

"We all are tempted, milady, even as the Lord Jesus Himself was when He walked the earth."

"Mr. Prindiville, you have spoken most correctly. My husband knew the old allurements at the beginning of our marriage but he never succumbed to their beckoning. He was absolutely wedded to the goal of shedding the past."

"Is the past all that he shed in those days, milady?" Prindiville asked wisely, hinting at what he dared not venture openly.

"No. . ." Elizabeth answered, hesitating. "No, it is not. I think Cyril disposed of his father at the same time, since Raymond Fothergill was such a strong link to, if not the source of, the behavior that threatened to bedevil him."

"So many years ago."

"Far too long, Mr. Prindiville, far too long. We are fortunate that a reconciliation occurred before Raymond's death."

"It was a beautiful moment, I am sure."

"You knew Raymond. What did you think of him?"

The man did not answer immediately. Elizabeth knew that she was placing him in a position that was hardly comfortable.

"Is it something you would prefer not to deal with?" she asked.

"If it is your wish that I do so, milady, how can I refuse?"

She found his formality not to be just an act, a mask as it were that he donned in her presence, but behavior that came from years of working with a family with whom he felt an unassailable bond, a formality out of respect, not just social expectation.

"It is my wish but only if it does not cause you distress," Elizabeth replied.

"I thought Raymond Fothergill was a man aching for forgiveness," he began. "An ache that he was certain would never be satisfied."

Elizabeth sucked in her breath, for what Roger Prindiville was saying mirrored what she had been thinking for a long time.

"Do you want me to proceed, milady?" he asked. "I meant nothing that would be—"

"Shush!" she interrupted, but with no harshness in her tone or manner. "Everything is fine. What we are doing is healthy, I think, a way of getting rid of cobwebs that should not have been allowed to gather in the first place."

Training her gaze again on the surrounding countryside that was caught in the deepening shadows of late afternoon and a slight mist, Elizabeth went on. "When it seemed that forgiveness was being denied my father-in-law by the entire family, I strongly suspected that he did go further down the decadent path he had been on for so long.

"For a time, his drinking seemed to offer solace, that and the women he paid to spend the night with him, but when these ran their course, and there was nothing left, I think the only thing that kept him going was the affection he received from those people he managed to help.

"Money was never to prove any sort of problem for Raymond Fothergill. He could spend his way through three lifetimes and still not bankrupt the fortune that had been at his disposal for all of his adult life."

"Could he have thought that the Lord was also withholding forgiveness?"

Elizabeth had considered that notion before, and had arrived at a conclusion she believed was inescapable.

"I think that that is likely, very likely," she admitted, "and this only made his life all the more tormented, another nail in the man's coffin, I imagine. One of many that have been driven into it over the years."

"You may be right, milady."

Elizabeth became weak and Prindiville reached out, putting his arm gently around her waist.

"The pain we cause one another," she whispered, "the needless pain."

From below, just outside the castle's main entrance, the shouts of one of the staff members could be heard. "*Someone is coming!*"

Elizabeth snapped out of her reverie and turned sharply in that direction, with Roger Prindiville doing likewise.

Two horses had just charged out from the wooded area northeast of the castle.

"I am not able to recognize either of the riders," Prindiville exclaimed, "but I can tell you that both are dressed like knights!"

Elizabeth and he hurried down the steps from the parapet, and to the castle's front entrance where two servants kept the heavy, oversized front doors open.

Prindiville asked her permission to summon the family's other guards, if necessary, and she consented. The horses were only a few hundred feet away by then. As soon as they had stopped, servants hurried over to the riders who had dismounted and offered to take the animals to the Fothergill stables.

"We need to see Lady Fothergill regarding a critically urgent matter," one of the knights said crisply.

A servant pointed to Elizabeth who had been joined by Clarice and Sarah. Standing with them was Roger Prindiville.

"Is he employed by the family?" the visitor asked.

"Yes, sir, he is. The man has been with this family for ages."

"And have you as well?"

"Indeed, sir. All of my adult life."

The knight slipped that servant, a man in his late fifties, a coin. And then he hurried up the pathway to where Elizabeth was standing.

"Lady Fothergill," he said, bowing before her, "my name

is Lofton, Erik Lofton. I am in the employ of Lord Nigel Selwyn."

"I have heard of him," she replied. "He is one who seems to prefer to be off by himself. I certainly respect his right to privacy though I could not live as he does."

"I have come about your husband," Lofton told her.

Elizabeth's hand closed around Roger Prindiville's arm.

"Is he alive?" she asked, her voice unsteady. "Have you been sent here to tell me that. . .or otherwise, Mr. Lofton?"

The blood had drained from her face as she spoke.

"Lord Fothergill is alive. . . ."

"Thank God!" she exclaimed. "Our prayers have been—"

"Milady?" Lofton cautiously interrupted.

"Yes? Is he injured then? Is that the bad news you have next to tell me?"

"I do not know if he is or not. But I know where he was when I left."

"You could not bring my husband back home?"

"He is in an underground maze, Lady Fothergill, at least I call it a maze, a series of tunnels and caverns at Woodhenge."

"Woodhenge is close, Mr. Lofton. We could be there in less than two hours."

"It would not be good at night, milady."

"You do not come here as a superstitious man, do you?" Elizabeth countered, interrupting him without apology. "Surely you are not going to be deterred by any of the long-ago goings-on at Woodhenge?"

He bowed fully and while still in that position, asked, "Would you permit me freedom to speak in order to save Lord Fothergill's life?"

Elizabeth's grip on Roger Prindiville's arm tightened.

"You have it, without threat of recrimination," she told him.

"The Druids are active again," Lofton declared as he rose to full height. "They have been conducting secret ceremonies at Woodhenge for some time now. Scores of babies, among other victims, have been sacrificed."

Clarice gasped, and she and Sarah had to hold onto one another.

"What does this have to do with Cyril. . .Lord Fothergill?" Elizabeth managed to ask though the words were difficult to form.

"He is in the underground area, as I have said. My comrade here, John Mottershead, and I tried to find him but the two of us failed. There are, it seems, countless twists and turns. That is why we have come—to get help, to send more men into the tunnel system with a plan, so that they will not simply become lost as it seems Lord Fothergill is."

"But can you be sure he is *still* there? Could Lord Fothergill perhaps have been taken elsewhere by his captors, if he were captured at all?"

"That is possible, milady."

Mottershead asked to be allowed to speak.

"Do so," Elizabeth told him.

"We have no other place to look," he said. "There is a reasonable likelihood that Lord Fothergill is lost, and just as much reason to think that he and the man with him are in no danger from any of the Druids."

"But how can you be sure?"

"Erik and I were compelled to kill all the Druids who were participating in a ceremony that we witnessed."

Sarah was becoming faint, the image of a field of slashed and bloody bodies too strong for her to endure without reacting as she did, her entire body trembling.

"I feel weak all of a sudden," she said in her thin, almost squeaky voice.

"Should you not be going inside, dear?" Elizabeth asked, her concern obvious. "I will tell you everything later."

Sarah shook her head.

"I will be all right," she replied.

"You should reconsider," her mother pressed, but Sarah would not be swayed.

"What this man is telling us concerns Father," she said. "I must hear it all firsthand, Mother."

Elizabeth told John Mottershead to continue.

"We cannot *eliminate* the possibility that one or two somehow escaped but that seems remote," he remarked. "We made quite certain that everyone was dead. It was a messy business but we were successful, I can assure you."

Roger Prindiville spoke up.

"Everyone you *saw*, is that not right?" he asked.

Erik Lofton did not like being questioned by a peer but he had to submit because Prindiville was with another lord. If they had worked for the same family, he might not have been as acquiescent.

"I must confess so."

"And if there were others you did not see, they either could have left Woodhenge altogether or gone into hiding underground," he said. "Am I so far from the mark?"

Lofton and Mottershead acknowledged that he might be hitting a bull's-eye.

"Lady Fothergill?" he asked. "May I recommend what we should do?"

"Whatever it takes, Mr. Prindiville," Elizabeth assured him. "I want you to be in charge."

"I did not intend to suggest anything of the sort," Prindiville, flustered, told her.

"I know that. You are a rather shy man, except when you were apprehending some criminals on the streets of London. You would not be so forward as to offer."

She took his hand in her own.

"But I know that you love my husband, and that he would appoint you himself if I were the one missing."

"It will take every guard on your staff," Prindiville said, "and these two strangers, if they be willing."

Both Erik Lofton and John Mottershead murmured their agreement to go along.

"Call the others now," Elizabeth ordered, "and let us get started."

"They are already on alert, milady. In not more than an hour, perhaps just over half that time, we can be on our way."

"I shall go with you," Elizabeth said resolutely.

"That would not be wise," Prindiville told her.

"It is my wish!"

"As you desire, Lady Fothergill," he acquiesced, not able to persist.

An embarrassed silence lasting a few seconds followed, until Clarice spoke up.

"Nor will my sister and I allow ourselves to be left behind either!" she declared, sharing Sarah's prior steadfastness.

It was their mother's turn to object.

"There might be great danger ahead," she advised them. "I think it is more prudent for the two of you to remain here."

"If that is what you will face, then it is what we must face also, Mother!" Clarice said. "And we *shall* do it together."

"Certain members of the staff will have to be armed," Prindiville added, noting that public lawlessness was increasing.

"See to it, Mr. Prindiville," Elizabeth said without hesitating.

CHAPTER 3

More than two dozen guards, some preferring horses, others on motorcycles, a few in cars, were on the road heading toward the site of the remains of Woodhenge, only forty minutes after Erik Lofton and John Mottershead arrived with their startling news. In just under ninety minutes they would be at the outskirts of the site. And they were as well-armed as a small army, with automatic rifles, handguns, and some grenades.

The urgency imposed by the passage of time made them travel at a brisk pace, though going at dusk did slow them down. And all were emboldened by a conviction that must have driven the knights involved in the very first Crusade centuries before, that they were setting out on a righteous mission and that Satan's forces ultimately would collapse.

It was well before the little caravan reached Woodhenge that, one by one, its members noticed something was wrong, very wrong.

Sarah was the first to speak but not to perceive the eerie state of the familiar countryside through which they were riding.

"No birds!" she exclaimed, her eyes widening as she surveyed the landscape on both sides of the road.

Normally there would be ravens or falcons or owls in evidence, particularly the latter, but all seemed to have disappeared.

"I did not notice," Elizabeth admitted naively. "Are you sure?"

Not as observant as Sarah had been, her mother and her sister peered closely at the countryside as she was speaking. The knights accompanying them had long before been aware of the absence of not just birds but other creatures, squirrels among them.

"Not on tree limbs or in the air or on the ground, looking for worms," Sarah continued, "or wherever else."

"Look, there. Gone!" she said, pointing in several directions. "And on the other side of this road, not a single one of them, no crows or sparrows or any other kind."

The others had been so intent on making it to the destination ahead as quickly as possible that they seemed to have shut out everything else, including their surroundings. But as soon as Sarah had spoken, all that changed dramatically, and any skepticism was discarded in an instant, replaced by curiosity and a growing, decidedly eerie feeling that thirty intelligent people might be heading into something far more demonic than any of them had had reason to suspect before they rode out from the Fothergill castle.

"No life. . ." Elizabeth observed nervously. "It seems as though we are traveling through some unmarked graveyard."

The descent of dusk did nothing but aid the mood that was seizing them, including the pseudo-knights who were, in most ways, the least fearful of men.

Mottershead rode his horse close to the Bentley.

"From what my relatives have told me since I was a young lad, every inch of this region had slipped into a similar state many centuries ago, and deviltry was rampant throughout, with the most heinous of acts committed perhaps daily," he addressed the women, "until the first wave of Christians was responsible for banishing the Druids."

"But why now?" Clarice asked. "How is it that they have returned to this day and age when they would seem to be less welcome than ever?"

Erik Lofton had been riding directly behind Mottershead.

"I think you should tell them," he said. "I think you should tell them what Lord Fothergill revealed to us."

"But can we take that liberty?" Mottershead called back to him.

"What if—?" the other knight started to say, then, glancing at Elizabeth and her two daughters, stopped himself.

But Mottershead had gotten the message.

"A time of evil. . ." he began.

And then he related to them everything that he knew. All three gasped at various stages, and Sarah had to close her eyes briefly.

"What hell my beloved has been through," Elizabeth said, the first to react.

"You are quite right, milady, a form of hell, a hint of hell is exactly what Lord Fothergill has experienced, I am sure," Mottershead agreed, "but all that will seem harmless in comparison if plans for the epidemic are not thwarted, an entire continent refashioned in Lucifer's own perverse and unholy image.

"And that *will* happen right down to the grotesque piles of burning bodies spewing suffocating smoke and foul, foul odors into God's clean air. So dense this will be—I can see it now—as to block out the sun from time to time, and joined, it shall be, by the pathetic moaning cries of the dying and those others who manage to escape death but find that life is far less desirable. The *kosmokratoras* will have an extraordinary time playing with *them!*"

He saw their blank expressions at the mention of the *kosmokratoras* and, apologizing, he then proceeded to explain to Elizabeth, Clarice, and Sarah the full significance of those creatures of darkness.

"Life then will make any survivors wish that they had died with the rest of the European population," he continued. "The *kosmokratoras* will *possess* those who are not Christians and mightily oppress those who are until it will be almost impossible to tell the difference."

"But Christians are indwelt by the Holy Spirit," Sarah said. "How could their behavior be changed so much?"

"Is every Christian living a life of sinless perfection?" he asked.

"I shan't think so," Elizabeth interpolated. "Only Christ was perfect. Only He became as we are in the flesh but without succumbing to any of our sins."

"Even so," Mottershead ventured, "Christians will be at

the mercy of those who are driven on and on by demons. Think of that, Lady Fothergill! Think of life so horrid that it seems inconceivable, a life of carnality and violence against the born and the unborn."

"And afterward God's judgment?" Elizabeth posed.

"That life may *be* His judgment for how we have debased His name for so long," he countered. "Think of the materialism of Christianity today, which has allowed the money changers to slip back into the temple.

"Think of the heartlessness toward those less fortunate, particularly orphaned children for whom the dwindling kindness of strangers is their only hope. What has happened to Christian charities? What has happened to—?"

Elizabeth was distressed with the knight's outlook.

"But my husband has never been that way," she protested, "nor was Raymond Fothergill, for that matter!"

Mottershead was not just stating an opinion or venturing some private prophecy as a kind of parlor game. He had come to be gripped by a prospect that was so terrifying that it quickly knotted up his stomach. But he soon regained control of himself and went on to tell the others what he thought the final outcome *could* be.

"There is the matter of total freedom for a vengeful devil, for this outcast from heaven," Mottershead added, "total freedom handed to him and his demons to do as they want with the ravaged humanity that would then exist all around them."

No one in that makeshift caravan was left untouched by the images stirred up by what the knight had told them, grisly scenes, scenes of such horror that they were tempted to turn and head back to the castle. They soon realized that, since demons were spirit and not of flesh and blood, those thick walls capable of keeping out man's armies would be like *papier-mâché* to any creatures from the underworld.

Frightened and sickened, Sarah grew paler than usual but somehow held up well enough as she listened. And Clarice seemed to take what this forthright knight named

John Mottershead had said with typical resiliency.

"Can anything be done?" Elizabeth asked.

"Edling, milady," Mottershead said, but with no sense of real hope. "It all rests on Edling's shoulders, I think. He will have to pull together all the political favors that are owed to him, that is, if he has the will to do anything at all."

About Edling there could be no resolute answer. This prime minister, not unlike others before him, was mercurial, which made him capable of towering displays of the greatest courage but also bouts of indecisiveness. However, the invisible looming nightmare of the hantavirus had brought out a sterner quality in this world leader. Whether his impulses were entirely noble on his part, arising out of concern for the survival of Britain itself, or more closely associated with saving his own hide, could not be fathomed by outsiders or by those individuals closest to No. 10 Downing Street. The Edling who responded to Cyril's visit was one that all Englishmen of noble or lowly birth would have admired. But, again an irony, few were to be allowed to know the reasons behind what would be his subsequent actions, actions meant to deal with the greatest calamity in European history. Soon Edling would be tested as never before. Adolfo had rebuffed the prime minister's chosen emissary, Lord Cyril Fothergill, a fact that it was doubtful Edling knew as yet, since the pope had not sent word, primarily out of pontifical pique that his meager spare time had been wasted on something as absurd as the premise of a worldwide epidemic instigated by Muslim extremists.

"As long as the crisis seems real," John Mottershead said, "there is good reason to believe that Edling will rise to the occasion. I hope that he is never seduced into thinking, as Adolfo was, that there is really no crisis at all."

CHAPTER 4

Woodhenge was just ahead.

When it had been in regular use by the Druid community, it was a center of activity, from the raising of crops to groups of people meeting there under the stars to study astronomy as well as astrology. And the sacrifices.

At first these were confined solely to animals. But, in time, the once peaceful, though always heretical Druid belief system was transformed, and infused with more violent precepts, including the substitution of human beings on altars of worship to the gods. That was when Woodhenge entered the most malevolent period of its existence, with scores, if not hundreds, of worshippers pouring into its confines, men and women who were now consumed by the need not of simple worship *per se* but a bloodlust so intense that it rivaled that of the ancient Romans. The latter had packed the Coliseum and the Circus Maximus solely for the thrill of seeing gladiators kill one another and lions, tigers, and other big cats devour Christians and anyone else considered a rebel against the Roman Empire.

"There was once hope that the growth of Christianity could have a leavening influence on Druidism," John Mottershead was saying. "But that did not happen, and I can imagine that the Druids of today are considerably more interested in reducing Christianity to rubble than in anything else."

The maniacal dedication implicit in those words chilled Elizabeth, Clarice, and Sarah and not a few of the guards with them.

To keep going, despite the life or death urgency of their mission, required major effort, and they all began to feel as though they were straining against actual physical barriers when, in fact, nothing of the sort blocked their path.

But that hardly mattered. All around them was the continuing evidence of the world they were entering, a world that seemed, in its way, wholly separate, a world of death and pain and despair for innocent men, women, and children, innocent babies, the signs everywhere: bones buried in a small forest; the absence of life of any kind of animal; land that was reaping the heritage of past centuries of homage to the prince of darkness.

"Just around the bend," Roger Prindiville announced, pointing directly ahead. "Am I not correct, Mr. Lofton?"

Erik Lofton agreed that they had finally arrived.

Smoke. . . .

Reaching well above the trees, its odor carried by night breezes, an odor that seemed to have an almost unholy taint.

But not only smoke.

The sounds. The *sounds* of crackling flames. The light, which was visible in flickering orange-red bursts that shimmered like bizarre dancing maidens.

"*Listen!*" Prindiville said.

Shrieking. Not quite human.

"How wicked that!" Elizabeth responded, recoiling from it. "Whatever it is cuts right through to the center of my soul."

"I have heard something like it one time in the Sudan, before I joined Lord Selwyn," Mottershead remarked.

"You were in Africa?" Sarah asked.

"I was, milady," the knight replied. "And my time there was taken up with many remarkable experiences."

"Was it voodoo, Mr. Mottershead?" Clarice, too, was interested.

One of the visitors to the Fothergill castle had been a missionary to Africa and he had many stories to tell about that ancient religion. She was anxious to hear more from this knight.

"Some form of it," Mottershead confirmed.

Clarice had been studying the different known ways Satan was able to deceive people into worshiping him. Her mother was curious as to why she had developed this interest, but

Clarice had no idea except that it was something she felt the Lord wanted her to do.

"Mr. Mottershead?"

"Yes, milady?"

"Were you able to see what was going on?"

"Briefly, and I thank God for such brevity."

"What happened?" Clarice persisted.

"I should not tell you."

"Am I so weak?"

"You are not so weak but you are so young."

"I am nineteen years old, Mr. Mottershead."

"It was a gruesome sight."

"I can endure your recollection, I assure you."

"But I cannot, milady."

He *had* put it out of his mind for many years, the sight of a man being skinned alive, and then his body, still living though barely, put into a large pot and boiled. The natives gathered around were shrieking at the sight of his agonized death throes, not out of remorse but delight.

Mottershead shook his head.

"I would very much like to drop this subject, milady, if you will permit me to do so."

She had been studying his face, looking into his eyes, and saw how horrible that glimpse into the past had been for him.

Dear Lord, Clarice thought, *I cannot put this man through whatever his ordeal was again. Forgive me for trying to do just that.*

She was about to say something to him when the horses began reacting nervously, one after the other neighing.

"Stop here," Prindiville said. "The Druids may not know that we have arrived just yet, though they are undoubtedly expecting us."

That was news to Elizabeth.

"Could they know about us at all?" she wondered naively. "How is that possible?"

"Undoubtedly they do know, milady," Erik Lofton told

her respectfully. "I have been half-expecting an attack for some time now."

Elizabeth was irritated at what she felt was an implicit unwillingness to discuss the matter with a woman.

"But I asked how, Mr. Lofton?" she repeated. "How could the Druids possibly know what is going on? I doubt very much that there is anyone among us who is a traitor for their cause."

He looked at her without blinking.

"Spies, milady," Lofton said.

"Where?" she asked. "Where could they be?"

Elizabeth's eyes suddenly darted almost comically from side to side.

"Along the road," Lofton replied.

"I have not seen any."

"Remember that woman hauling buckets of water?"

Elizabeth did recall seeing her, and feeling not a little pity for the woman.

"But she was so poor, Mr. Lofton, dressed in the worst of rags, dirty-faced. Any of us could see that."

She paused, trying to make him feel uncomfortable as she confronted him with a logical question: "How could you suspect someone like that of being a spy?"

"May I say that she *could* have been more than just ordinary, milady," Mottershead then said. "That would be the genius of any attempt at spying by the Druids, you know. How effective could they become if their spies stood out?"

He waited, for effect, and then went on.

"Their spies would have to fit in, of course, or their value would be eliminated. So, I suspect that the Druids were busy converting local people to their beliefs, and have been using them to alert those involved in sacrifices of any danger coming their way."

"Have been? You think this might have been going on for some time?"

"What we both saw, Erik and I, could not have been organized overnight. They obviously have been doing this for some time. And the buried bodies of children that we noticed were not recent but had been there for months."

"What else have you seen, Mr. Mottershead?" Elizabeth asked.

He tried hard to choose his words carefully.

"We are taught much like the knights of medieval times to be on alert, during times of great crime and violence," he said, "to be aware of every detail. Some of us, after many years, have been known to become sloppy perhaps, but that instinct never completely dies."

Clarice questioned him this time.

"And you have noticed some clues other than that one poor woman as we have traveled?" she asked.

"I have."

Given the opportunity now, Mottershead launched into a list of these.

"I noticed some men talking as they stood at a crossroads soon after we started," he said. "When we came within their sight, they scurried away, but one of them, possibly the leader, twice glanced over his shoulder at us."

"But if Druids are so intent on keeping themselves unnoticed, why were *they* so obvious?" Clarice asked reasonably.

"To anyone but a knight, what I saw would seem commonplace. I focused attention on what happened within the course of a few seconds. Nobody else would have noticed."

"Was there more?"

"A man sitting on his front porch, with a horse standing to one side, eating some grass. That little vignette looked very casual, repeated there and elsewhere throughout England every day of every week of every month of every year."

"Then what alerted you, Mr. Mottershead?" Clarice asked, not sure what the knight was getting at.

He went on, smiling tolerantly. "I turned a moment later and looked back, and saw that he had mounted the horse and was running off in the general direction we were headed but by another route that would not intersect with our apparent one."

"And there have been other incidents?"

Elizabeth was astounded at how much she had been unaware of, if what this knight were saying was to be believed.

"More indeed, milady."

Still he seemed reluctant to divulge the details.

"I am not someone who will become hysterical when presented with reality, Mr. Mottershead," Elizabeth remarked icily.

She paused, looking at him with a sharply disapproving expression. "I am not afraid of mice, either."

"Forgive me, Lady Fothergill," the knight apologized. "Not everyone I meet is as involved or alert as you."

Elizabeth's temper flared.

"Not every *woman*, is that what you mean?"

Mottershead knew that she had seen through his politeness.

"I am afraid so, milady. Please excuse my manner."

But Elizabeth relented because she suddenly felt guilty about being as harsh as she had been with a stranger, someone who seemed interested only in getting her husband back safely.

"It is I who should tender an apology," she told him. "Cyril has been gone too long. Suddenly you appear with the most horrible stories. And here we are, armed to the teeth and hoping we are acting quickly enough to save his life.

"Am I distraught?" Elizabeth asked, smiling thinly. "I suppose one could say that."

"I shall continue then?" he asked deferentially.

"You shall, Mr. Mottershead."

"There have been signals along the way at every turn, almost from the start, it seems, and never letting up, either."

He pointed behind them.

"Just a few minutes ago, I saw someone on one side of the road signal to someone else hiding behind trees on the other, a sudden movement of the head, not simple nodding or shaking but another quite different gesture, and this motion was reciprocated by the second individual."

Mottershead cleared his throat.

"And there were the children I saw in a tree house surveying us as we passed by," the knight added, his tone cryptic.

"Children as spies?" she remarked incredulously. "The Druids do not stop at using innocent children in this awful business?"

Elizabeth was seeing more than ever how cloistered her life in and around the family castle really had been. Whatever information or news as such that she received was provided by servants, visiting friends, or her family. She had no real independent source.

"They do," the pseudo-knight assured her. "No age group is off-limits, milady. Whoever serves their purpose."

"I think as loathsome as the idea is, it should not be completely unexpected by any of us," Clarice admitted.

"Why do you say that, milady?" John Mottershead asked.

"The nature of children."

"Their curiosity, you mean?"

"That and the fact that they cannot be *forced* to do whatever it is that they are just not interested in doing."

Mottershead caught the essence of where she was heading.

"And knights like us would spark their interest."

"Children would be fascinated, in any event, by a caravan led by two knights in shining armor, plus motorcycles and two cars," Clarice, so young herself, agreed. "They would not have any trouble obeying a command to keep track of everybody here."

"That is certainly true," Mottershead acknowledged, "and how effective they are. As soon as we passed by, these little children scampered down a ladder and hurried over to several adults who had come out of a modest dwelling near that large tree."

"What happened then?" Clarice asked, fascinated.

"The last I saw, the young ones were gesturing wildly, and the five adults seemed especially disturbed."

Clarice fell into silence, no longer disrupting the knight's observations.

"But it was hardly just what I saw," he added, still on the alert, ready for any clue that hinted at danger.

"You *heard* some clues, Mr. Mottershead?" Sarah spoke this time. "I have not noticed anything unusual."

"Calls supposed to sound as though they were coming from birds or dogs or cows were not from these sources at all, I told myself. . .they turned out to be rather poor imitations, frankly."

He chuckled as he remarked, "It was not hard to tell the difference. These were unequivocally man-made."

The shrieks were continuing, from ahead of them and it sounded as though other voices had joined in.

Africa. . .at night. . .tribal members standing guard. . . sounds from animals heard by few Englishmen before. . .but then the others, not from four-legged creatures but another source altogether, perhaps not even a human one.

Prindiville ordered one of the guards to scout the wooded area ahead of them.

"Do nothing foolish," he said. "And return as soon as you can. We are prepared to act as soon as you do."

The man nodded and crossed the road, entering the wooded area.

"We can guide you to where the entrance to the underground system is," Lofton advised. "Should we not head straight for it?"

"Not until my scout returns. I want to know what we will be facing. Some could be hiding, if there are any left at all, but I need to know if the scout finds *anybody*. Just one Druid is sure indication there are likely to be others undercover or underground."

A direct attack, ah, that would have been thrilling, just like the old days when knights charged into battle against the Muslims, weapons flashing, battle cries issuing from them would have been satisfying for both men. Yet to do this, to hit any remaining group of Druids head-on, would have meant certain death for Erik Lofton and John Mottershead, though they might have been able to kill a dozen or more of the cult members. But they were not successful in finding Cyril Fothergill and Henry Letchworth.

Prindiville's cynicism was unvarnished.

"You are here but Lord Fothergill and another man are not?" he said. "How convenient!"

The tone was insinuating but Mottershead wisely chose to ignore this.

"We both were out of sight, Mr. Prindiville. The Druids never knew about the two of us, mostly because we entered carefully and retreated in the same manner. We *have* learned to be careful when we are hiding. When we attacked, the factor of absolute surprise was overwhelming."

Between such men, doing the work of knights without being called such, there remained often a bit of rivalry or one-upmanship, and this has been going on ever since the original orders of knights had been established. The verbal jesting could be vicious but, finally, when it was over, the bond that existed between them remained unbroken.

Prindiville's expression was changing.

"Discretion being the better part of valor, I assume."

Mottershead was bracing himself for another round of questioning.

"Something like that."

But Prindiville smiled as he said, "I would not have acted differently."

"That is enormous comfort to me," John Mottershead told the guard with just a dash of sarcasm.

CHAPTER 5

Hooded men held them prisoner in one of the underground caverns. Only four women were left. The others had been taken, their screams and the smell of smoke evidence of what had happened. Cyril and Henry did their best to protect the women but were overwhelmed by Druids, each of whom possessed superior strength.

"One by one. . ." Fiona Fothergill observed. "Until none of us is left, and our babies' souls will be transferred into other bodies."

"They are under satanic delusion," Cyril told her. "There is no truth to soul transference. It is a lie from the deceiver himself, the prince of lies."

"My baby will go to heaven then?" Fiona asked pitiably.

Her concern never had been as much for herself as for her unborn child. She wanted to give birth and hold him in her arms and be his mother for the rest of her life. But now it seemed that she would never have a chance.

"Your baby will be in the company of angels the instant his mortal life is over," Cyril assured the nineteen-year-old.

"You are like your father Raymond," Fiona said, meaning no offense, as she rejoiced at that assurance. "That man was kind to my mother. He—"

"But if I had been the father," Cyril interrupted, "I would have married her or otherwise provided for the two of you rather than let you both continue walking the dark, cold streets of a city like London, engaging in a degrading practice.

"Tell me this, Fiona: How was my father being kind in his treatment of your mother and you? Is letting you go on the way you have been an act of compassion or kindness but not one of indifference?"

At home, if he were as angry as that, Cyril would have pounded his fist against the paneled wood of the expansive room that served as his den, for him the most private place in the entire rambling castle. But the jagged rock wall of that cavern made such a display dangerous and so he was reduced to sputtering.

"You do *not* have the pain he did," she replied.

Cyril needed to be convinced that, except at the end, his father was anything but a rounder, a wealthy rounder who bedded down whatever women struck his fancy and then left them behind a day or a week or, at most, a month later.

"What pain is that?" Cyril asked, his contempt for anything she said and a deep skepticism hardly disguised, especially to someone such as Fiona who was adept at reading the emotions played across someone's face.

Fiona Fothergill hesitated, as before, when she had been reluctant to tell him her name, knowing that learning of it would greatly upset him.

"For a short time, desperate for companionship, Raymond became. . .he. . .he became—"

She threw her head back.

"You do not want to know the rest," she assured him with a bravado that seemed to come to her quite naturally.

"Another terrible revelation?" he snorted. "You should know that my father and I reconciled before his death. I no longer hold any ill will toward him or his memory."

Fiona smiled, showing a wisdom that was unusual for any teenager, a wisdom that only years of seeing the dark side of man's nature could instill, equal parts cynicism, bitterness, and a prevailing hopelessness, but also a wisdom stripped of pretension.

"None whatever, Lord Fothergill?" Fiona asked. "Dare you say that?"

"I dare to say whatever it is that I wish because my standard is truth," he declared, "truth and *only* that!"

"And mine is not?"

That was not the right question to ask since answering it hardly required some intellectual leap for him.

"You have no standards whatsoever that I can see," Cyril

told the young woman. "Is that answer enough?"

"Judging by those standards that you have pursued during your life, I gather. But then what made *yours* so special, Lord Fothergill? So special that you saw fit to turn your back self-righteously on your father?"

"Your very life is a lie!" he yelled.

"Because I am not as *respectable* as you?"

"You do not know the meaning of respectability," Cyril said. "It has *not* been bred into you for hundreds of years. Who are *your* ancestors? Barmaids, I suppose. And stable sweepers."

Fiona stood, placing her hands on her hips.

"We *are* damaged goods," she acknowledged to Cyril, but also addressing Henry and the other women, "and second-rate ones at that. The upper class is usually served by certain women of elegance, with their pampered bodies, including the sweetest-smelling rare perfumes on their skin, and imported clothing that they wear with a swirl to their step and a haughtiness in the way they hold their heads up."

She sneered at herself and the others.

"Some like us are born in dirty alleys among the rest of the garbage," she continued. "It is a miracle when we avoid disease as well as we do."

The other women murmured their agreement.

"We have lived the years that we have without starving either," she said, "though hunger is hardly unknown among us."

. . .*when we avoid disease as well as we do.*

Those words chilled Cyril because he wondered if the Muslims and the Druids had thought of using prostitutes as well as common rats to spread the hantavirus. Women of the night were plentiful in every major city, certainly in London, Paris, and even Rome. And they were frequented by poor farmers as well as men of noble birth.

She faced Cyril and Henry, though not with contempt.

"But were even my kind meant to die like this?" she asked of the two men. "At the hands of butchers?"

Cyril stepped in.

"At the hands of demons!" he declared. "That is more likely. God would never sanction anything like that!"

Fiona confronted him.

"But we deserve it, do we not?" she said. "Could this be the punishment that God has handed down to us? For those who turn their backs on His Son, Jesus Christ, this is not punishment at all. It is a trifle compared to what eternity will hold."

She lowered her voice and a marked melancholy took over it.

"Where the fires will burn ceaselessly but not consume, giving us pain but not oblivion. . ." she muttered.

"That *is* hell," Cyril said.

"And we shall enter it all too soon."

"You need not. You could stand at the gates of heaven and be welcomed by a holy and forgiving Father."

"Father. . ." Fiona said wistfully. "My daddy was any man who kept me for more than a few days."

"Aye," each of the others said.

A second later, one added zestfully, "Why, I thought I had died and gone to heaven when that happened."

They chuckled briefly, foolishly, then were quiet.

Fiona stood before Cyril.

"You speak of being welcomed by God."

She turned around twice.

"Look at me!" she said. "I am worse than worthless. My anonymous customers throw me a few shillings and I am theirs, my body owned by them for whatever time they have paid. But then the money is gone, it is spent for bread and some meat from time to time, a night's lodging somewhere, and a secondhand dress.

"And then I must take to the streets again, and walk the cobblestones or the asphalt yet another time, until the next one like some mad sculptor carves out pieces of me.

"But I have deserved this, I know that, sir, and that is, I think, why I have continued since I was a child."

"A child?" Henry spoke finally. "You have been making your way like this since you were a child?"

That women would sell their bodies was unsettling enough to him, for his thoughts were of a purity that few men knew. But that this could begin when they were ten or twelve years old was particularly appalling.

"Yes!" she said, neither proud nor ashamed, but resigned to a life that seemed as natural to her and the others as breathing the air around them, London air, filled with the odors of ancient times.

"It is a way, *my* way of *continuing* the punishment that I am being dealt," she added, "*if God ever decided to stop!*"

She had been looking at Henry as she spoke.

"You are an innocent man," she said, suddenly blushing. "Forgive me for saying these things. I see your goodness and it makes me ashamed. I am not often ashamed, you know. You make me feel that way. And I do not know why."

She fell at his feet. But Henry would not allow her to stay there and reached down, gently pulling her to a standing position.

"It is not I," he said softly. "It is the Holy Spirit seeking entrance."

"Men have been after me for a long, long time," she said wearily.

"It is time for you to shut them out, and let Someone else in."

She turned to Cyril for a moment.

"There is something else you should know about your father," she said.

"What is it, Fiona?" he asked, steeling himself.

"The Druids. . ." she said, still not looking up at him. "Your father saved my mother from becoming one of their sacrifices."

Cyril realized that, in spite of their soul-deep reconciliation before his father's death, there was more that he could learn about the lost years, years in which there was no contact at all between them.

"She was about to die in one of their wickermen?"

"She was."

"How did he stop this from happening?"

This time, lifting her head, her gaze met his.

"Raymond was able because—"

She clearly did not want to say what Cyril was waiting to hear.

"It is all right," Henry whispered, his lips close to the young woman's ear. "You can tell us anything you want."

"Where was my father that he could do this? Did he accidentally stumble upon one of their ceremonies?"

"Because he had become one of them!"

She hung her head and Henry put his hand on the back of her neck, trying to comfort the young woman.

For Cyril, learning that his father was once a Druid proved as hard to take as discovering that Raymond Fothergill had fathered a child by a prostitute.

She could see the shock that registered on his face.

"He was so lonely," Fiona went on, "and the Druids seemed to offer him what he could not get elsewhere."

Cyril knew what she was saying, and his old regrets came to the surface after being ignored for so long.

"At first they presented themselves as merely a group of rather quaint people who were gathering together and worshipping in a strange but harmless way," she recalled. "Raymond ignored the conflicts that existed between Druidism and his own Christian beliefs, at least in the beginning."

Instinctively she reached out and touched Henry's hand.

"Then he saw the violence of their sacrifices, the evil of these, committed against helpless babies, against defenseless women. One of these was my mother. He could not tolerate that. He grabbed her and they ran away."

"Where did my father and your mother go?" Cyril asked.

"Raymond's wealth made it unnecessary for them to hide away in shacks on isolated strands of land near the coast. He bought my mother a small house just south of the Scottish border, near a village where he had some acquaintances who promised to look out for her. And he paid them well to do that."

"Did the Druids leave them alone?" Cyril asked.

"They tried to hunt him down soon after he took my mother from them but they never succeeded. Raymond was too clever. And he had help, from noblemen and poor wretches alike."

Some pride showed on her face.

"He was more than a match for the lot of them. And there were his angels. They protected him and my mother."

The affection and the loyalty that Raymond commanded had not ceased to amaze his son.

"And what happened to their relationship?" Cyril asked Fiona.

"I never found out," she told him. "They drifted apart, the visits ceased, and my mother and I were left alone."

"Did you hate him for this?"

"At first, when I was old enough to understand, I did, oh, how strong my hatred was for that man, and how much it grew the more I comprehended what he had done. Even now, I cannot explain what happened to him. You told me that you spent the last hours of his life with him. Can you let me know anything?"

Cyril sadly shook his head.

"When my mother died, and I took to the streets, I think what I wanted most of all was to run into him. I wanted to get revenge."

Fiona spoke in a low voice, and seemed almost casual. But Cyril found that admission startling.

"You would have gone to bed with your father?"

"And then told him afterward my name."

"The man would have been destroyed!" Cyril exclaimed. "I think he might have taken his own life."

"But that was what I sought, a chance to get back at him, to taste sweet revenge, to watch him recoil in guilt and loathing."

"But you never did? Tell me that you never did."

"I did not ever go to bed with Raymond Fothergill though I. . .I—"

She was starting to cry.

"I saw him one night. The fog was especially bad then. I had my usual station. But there were no customers that night except—"

"My father?"

"Yes. . . ."

"But I thought you said—"

"He *wanted* to be a customer, Lord Fothergill, but I did not sell him any merchandise. He promised me more money for one night than I had earned in a month."

"But you refused?"

"I refused."

"Did you know who he was?"

"Did I, Lord Fothergill? I surely did, from the first moment I saw him I knew, coming out of the fog as he did toward me."

"But you wanted revenge. You admitted that just now. What stopped you? Surely my father could not have recognized you after so many years of being away."

"He never did, you are right. I could not do what I had wanted to do for so long because I saw how spent he looked, old, slightly stooped over, his hair grayer than I had remembered, the circles under his eyes puffy, his skin pale and wrinkled, veins showing through. And there was a desperation about him."

"A desperation?" Cyril asked dumbly. "I have no idea what you mean by that, Fiona."

"I think he knew he was nearing death. And yet there he was, still alone, with no one even to hold his hand. If the only way he could get companionship of a sort was to pay for it, then he would do just that. He had the money."

Cyril groaned at the image of his father that Fiona Fothergill was presenting, and he would have liked to scoff at its insinuations, to call the nineteen-year-old prostitute a liar, true to her way of life, and once they were free of Druid captivity, turn his back on her, and walk away without acknowledging her existence again.

But he knew that she was speaking the truth.

"Is there anything else?" he asked.

"When I refused his offer, he nodded, wished me a good night, and walked away, disappearing back into the fog."

She wiped away the tears but more came coursing down her cheeks.

"But then I thought I might spend a little time with him, just talk a bit, and not charge him for this, I would never have asked him for anything but those few moments.

"And so I quickly walked after him. I shouted, 'Lord Fothergill. . . .' He walked a few more feet but after I called after him a second time, he stopped as though someone had hit him, and, turning, faced me; my father faced me for the last time.

"He never asked how I knew his name. He just sighed, that was all he did, sighed once, and I could see, in his eyes, the approach of death, the fear that he would die alone, in some strange place, with no one to care about him, no one even to know who he was."

"That sounds like someone I met a few days ago."

"Loneliness is a terrible thing."

"And you have been very lonely, I imagine."

"I was looking forward to having the company of my child in a few months."

"Any idea of the identity of the father?"

She tried to put on a hard facade but failed.

"He could be a wealthy businessman," she said, her voice rough-edged with emotion, "or a close advisor to Edling, or a score of others. I have no way of knowing. . . ."

Her eyes were filling with tears again.

"But at least I would have a child," Fiona went on. "At least I could hold something precious and innocent in my arms."

"But what sort of life would you give him?"

"Not a very good one, sir. I would have eventually given

my baby up for adoption. Some barren couple would pay good money for any child of mine."

She patted her stomach.

"He wants to see his mother," she said. "He is tired of all that darkness. He wants to leave my body and look up into my face and cry for attention."

She looked nervously at the small opening to the cavern.

"But *they* are coming back. And my dream, this one decent dream of mine that somehow has lasted, will be slashed from me and burnt on some evil altar."

CHAPTER 6

The guard who had been sent ahead to scout the scene finally returned.

Named Paul Ladley, he had been with the Fothergills nearly as long as Roger Prindiville. He was shorter than the other guards, his face boyish but not without scars and blemishes.

Visibly tremulant, he stood before the two knights, guards, and the Fothergill women.

"I must report—" he began but choked on his words. He seemed to be struggling to remain on his feet.

Prindiville walked over to him.

"We have seen the worst of conditions as bobbies in London, Paul, you and I have," he declared with insight that only another veteran could muster. "Can there possibly be something ahead as bad as your reaction indicates, my comrade?"

Ladley's face contorted as he recalled what he had reconnoitered.

"Oh, I think it is, Roger, it is indeed," the other man managed to say, though his face lacked its usual strength. "When we fought criminals anywhere else, I knew that I was being opposed by mere flesh and blood. You know for a surety that I am hardly a man of ready cowardice, for I could withstand whatever the other side might wage against me, and charge ahead through their lines, decimating them left and right."

"What is the difference this time?" Prindiville asked, showing great patience, his sympathy for this man unambiguous.

Ladley looked into his face.

"Nothing *human!*" he exclaimed. "Not even the most depraved madness could do what I saw back there."

Prindiville turned and asked Elizabeth if his friend could sit down in their Bentley and get himself together.

"Of course," she said without hesitation.

After Ladley was seated, Prindiville stood outside the car.

"Are you able to tell us more?" he asked.

Ladley nodded, and, after coughing a couple of times, went on to describe what he had seen in the clearing where Lofton and Mottershead had killed six Druids earlier.

Women.

"Four of them. . ." he said, still having a hard time.

"Female Druids?" Prindiville inquired.

"*Not Druids!*" Ladley cried out. "These were sacrifices, Roger. Oh, these eyes of mine saw it all! Those helpless women were being *attacked—!*"

Prindiville, ever mindful of Elizabeth, Clarice, and Sarah who were listening, silently prayed that Ladley would exercise discretion.

"The women were pregnant, Roger. Those monstrous creatures wanted the babies for sacrifice in a wickerman!"

Ladley described tersely how all four perfectly shaped little bodies were alive, and squirming, when they were placed into a wickerman.

"One baby instinctively reached out for something to hold onto, and closed his hand around a finger of one of the Druids," Ladley continued.

"Did that not give the man pause?" Prindiville asked. "Could his heart have been so cold as to reject—?"

"*No, no, it did not!*" the other man said. "Do you know what he did to those fingers? Do you—?"

Even Roger Prindiville turned white as he shook his head.

And then the babies were placed inside the wickerman, none of them moving much, their eyes still closed, and none realizing that their mother's womb no longer offered them any protection.

"A fire was started at its base," he continued, "consuming them in seconds."

Sarah gagged as she swallowed and buried her head in her hands. Clarice bit her lower lip, and tried to continue paying attention but could not, and leaned against her sister, the two of them quietly sobbing.

With great effort, Elizabeth managed to avoid succumbing to a fainting spell. She was absorbed, unable to turn away, while unaccustomed to such brutality.

Only so short a distance from where we live, she told herself. *How many ceremonies have been there without us ever knowing about them? This is England, not some foreign land where barbaric actions are routine.*

But the babies were only part of the infamy.

"And what happened to the mothers?" she asked, her voice tense.

"Those creatures, those men, but I wondered how they could be human at all. . .they—" Ladley attempted to reply.

"What men would do this?" Elizabeth persisted.

"Druids, yes, their faces partially obscured by hoods, men with dark eyes narrowed intently—"

"What happened to the women, Mr. Ladley?" she repeated.

"They were thrown into a large hole that must have been dug soon after Lord Selwyn's knights left."

Prindiville took over the questioning again.

"And the other bodies," he asked, "what became of those?"

"Other bodies?" Ladley repeated dumbly.

"Yes, the Druids that Erik and John here dispatched. Did you see them?"

Ladley had seen these all right.

"Into the same pit. Just like that, Mr. Prindiville, human beings treated like some other day's garbage."

He could scarcely believe fellow Druids would be treated in so unfeeling a manner by their survivors.

"There were no last words or rites or anything like that," he said, knowing what he saw but still disbelieving the evidence his eyes had presented.

"And what then?" Prindiville questioned.

"They hauled in a huge makeshift chest, and. . .and they

released. . .they. . .they brought in and released—"

Ladley was in worse shape than before.

"Speak up, man!" Prindiville pressed. "Spit it out!"

"*Rats!*" he screamed.

Paul Ladley was ashamed of the way he was acting but he simply was not able to contain his emotions.

"Hundreds of rats feeding—"

His eyes gave some indication of the terror felt by his soul.

"And the Druids, the stinking, inhumane Druids, just sat there and. . .and watched, watched and laughed while in back of them, amid the flames—!"

Knights could show their feelings in front of other knights but not before the people they were sworn to protect. Yet what Ladley had witnessed was so appalling that he could not dam the tide.

. . . .*the Druids, the stinking, inhumane Druids just sat there and. . .and watched, watched and laughed.*

Prindiville shook the other man.

"You must not go on weeping like this," he said sternly. "We need your help, Paul. Do not let us down."

"My help?" Ladley repeated. "I am no good to anyone now, Roger."

"But of course you are, laddie," Prindiville tried to reassure him. "I would not be wasting my time on you if I felt that that was all there was left of you."

Ladley shook his head.

"You *are* wrong about me. Can you not see that, Roger? We fight not against flesh and blood this night."

"We can take on the demons of hell itself if the Lord be with us," Prindiville reminded his friend. "We are doomed only if we forget that, and fail to go to our knees before a holy God, asking Him for the courage to fight this fight. Go with me now, dear comrade, and we shall pray together."

Ladley nodded slowly and stepped out of the Bentley, and knelt side by side with the other man.

Everyone else followed their example, and went to their

knees, clasping their hands together in prayer.

It was then that they heard the loudest shriek of all, as though it came from a giant unseen beast that had been wounded and was sounding forth its rage and pain, as well as its defiance.

"Now this is how I think we should go about rescuing Lord Fothergill," Roger Prindiville addressed the twenty-five guards. "Do I have everybody's attention?"

With no one questioning his position of leadership, especially Elizabeth Fothergill who knew of her husband's respect and affection for the man, Roger Prindeville told them of his plan, and when he was finished, all agreed that it seemed the only one possible. They would go down into the underground system of caverns and stay together. If they split up and went in different directions in groups of, say, three or four, they might encounter a force of Druids of much greater size, and could not adequately defend themselves, and, one by one, each would be killed until none was left.

"We must be as heavily armed as humanly possible, but not enough to restrict our movements," he told the other Fothergill guards as well as Erik Lofton and John Mottershead. "The more weapons they see us with, the more intimidated they will be. I am hoping that they will offer no resistance and simply surrender."

Prindiville tended to think of the Druids as menacing, yes, but otherwise primitive in their knowledge and abilities.

"They are but farmers, simple people of the land, and not fearsome warriors," he told the knights. "They raise their crops and their children, living and dying on the same acreage for generations past and to come."

"But since that is so, are we not essentially on *their* land?" John Mottershead, stepping forward, pointed out.

"You may be right."

"Well, then, Mr. Prindiville, have you ever seen a fiercer individual than someone defending his land against intruders? Surely you can understand that such a man is a warrior in all but the name."

Prindiville considered that for a moment.

"You speak with wisdom. But in such a case, it is not dedication or vigor that is important but the weapons he has at his disposal. A pitchfork is a poor alternative to a grenade."

"Unless you happen to be standing just a few feet from your enemy. In that case, I would take the pitchfork *above* the grenade."

"But what if I *also* had a sword and could whack off your head in a single sweep, something I have been well trained to do, whereas the only instrument that the farmer uses the pitchfork for is to pitch hay, as the name suggests? And if fighting quarters were too confined for either weapon, I could then resort to my dagger, could I not?"

Prindiville could see that Mottershead was uncomfortable having his viewpoint shredded mercilessly.

"But it does not end there, this matter, my dear man," he said.

He smiled knowingly.

"And if this farmer of yours, armed with that pitchfork you mention," he added, "is forced to face three or four experienced guards, where would the odds be then, Mr. Mottershead? With a simple farmer who typically faces nothing more violent than two of his hogs fighting? Or those men who, between them, have killed enough of the enemy, wherever and whoever that enemy happened to be, to fill several large graveyards?"

The other man returned his smile.

"*Touché*," he said.

Elizabeth was considering something else as she had been listening to the exchange between the two men.

What if that conjectured farmer, she thought, *is being aided by demons from the pit of hell? What are the odds then? Could it be that these people now are not the original farmers but have been replaced, by a group of Druids who intend to spread into surrounding farms, taking those over as well? Will they be the ones to inherit twentieth century England just before the millennium?*

She did not speak of this to anyone.

They decided to go *around* the wooded area at its southern point, coming in on the clearing from the east, north, and west, which would place them *behind* any Druids left to guard the entrance to the system.

"Those devils probably are expecting us from the south," Prindiville reasoned. "We must surprise them if possible."

On the road bordering the wooded area, Prindiville left behind three men just in case. One of these was Paul Ladley.

"I *can* go with you and the others," the guard protested. "I feel much better now, stronger. The Druids could throw against me whatever they wanted, and I would not buckle; I hope you believe that, Roger."

Prindiville sympathized but thought that the other man should be stationed at the location where engagement with the enemy was least likely.

"Trust me," he asked of Ladley. "Your being here instead of going below with us is a precaution. This is an evil we encounter that no one has come up against before now. The women cannot be left unprotected."

"I shall give my life for the three of them, if necessary," Ladley told him, fully prepared to do no less than that.

"I can count on no man more completely than you, Paul."

The other guard seemed to want to say something more but was reluctant.

"Tell me what you wish but hurry," Prindiville urged.

"Come back," Ladley said simply but with the deepest feeling.

Prindiville patted him on the shoulder and grinned.

"I shall do just that," he agreed, "if the good Lord Himself should decide to send me this way again."

"Roger?"

"Yes?"

"Are you *ready* for what I saw?"

Ladley's heart beat faster at just the suggestion of those images.

"It was worse than you said, was it not?" Prindiville asked, knowing the sort of man his comrade was.

"How could you tell?" Ladley asked, his face frozen.

"I know you as I would a brother if I had one."

"It was, Roger," answered Ladley, "it was so much worse that I could not describe the rest, or, if made to do so, I might have gone quite mad."

"I am not sure I *can* stand it, you know. I have always prized being in control of myself."

Ladley threw up his hands.

"No one knows about that except the Lord Himself. But we all sense, I know, that you are the better Christian here, Roger. And the men will be emboldened by your example, in their faith *and* their actions."

"I think I am not better at all. I talk better perhaps, a little bluster here and there in the name of the Lord. Sometimes I might act a shade better, watching my mouth and what words escape it, especially in front of the women. But the rest of the time, I remain like every other man here, if anything worse than some."

Prindiville shook his head resignedly as he considered those *other* occasions.

"Pray for us. . ." he said, the faintest hint of plaintiveness in his voice.

"Without ceasing."

Prindiville turned to go and rejoin the other men who were waiting for him less than twenty feet away.

"Roger?"

"Yes, Paul."

"I covet your prayers as well."

"You have them."

"Good-bye, my brother," Ladley said. "May there be angels at your side."

Roger Prindiville spoke with hope that was not altogether genuine.

"Have they ever left?"

And then he and the other guards headed across the road into the valley of the shadow.

CHAPTER 7

And my dream, this one decent dream of mine that somehow has lasted, will be slashed from me on some evil altar. . . .

"Your dream shall not die," Cyril declared to Fiona Fothergill.

"If it does not," she said, "I pledge to bow before your Christ and ask that His blood wash my sins away so that I might be forgiven before Him."

"You must not bargain with God, young lady," he told her.

"But a bargain is what I strike, Lord Fothergill, and that is the way it shall be. I know no other way from this life of mine. Can you expect something else from my kind?"

Her impudent nature distanced Cyril more than she realized but this was not without a struggle. He had turned his back on her father, and now that he was close to turning his back on Fiona herself, he despised the likelihood. But there was no time to search his soul on this matter.

Footsteps. . . .

"Fight!" he told the women as he spread his legs slightly, speaking with a defiance born of his recent experiences.

"Why should we do that?" Fiona asked. "We might fall or be kicked in the stomach, and get our babies hurt."

"If you do not *immediately* create some kind of diversion, and a phony fight is the only one that might work, then more than hurt is going to befall those poor little ones, remember that, all of you!" he retorted.

Fiona nodded, and told the others that they might as well trust him, so fight was what they would do, a fight serving the secondary purpose of expunging the frustration they felt as well as some of the panic over being held prisoner.

The three Druids entering the cavern did not see Cyril on one side of the entrance and Henry on the other, each gripping a rock. Instead their attention was centered on the four women who had started a brawl that was wild enough to be realistic. They had only the women and their unborn children in mind, and were careless of anyone else as a result. Two of the Druids went down together, their skulls cracked open. The third managed to duck out of the way and quickly withdrew a dagger from a brown sheath on his belt. But he never had a chance to use it. One of the women jabbed a long, straight hairpin through the Druid's neck, the point coming out the other side. The man staggered as he reached one hand behind his head, and tried to pull it out, the other hand flailing wildly. Groaning, he fell forward, against Henry.

"His eyes!" Henry exclaimed as he stepped aside and the Druid hit the stone floor. "They were filled with such black loathing, such—"

He doubled his hands into fists as he looked from woman to woman.

"They will *not* take your babies!" he declared to the four. "I would give up my own life to prevent that from happening."

Three of the women were motionless but Fiona walked up to him.

"You cannot mean what you just said," she remarked. "We are strangers to you and Lord Fothergill, and I am but a prostitute."

She backed away from him.

"Do not look at me that way," she begged him.

"What did you see in my eyes?" Henry asked her, honestly unaware. "Just now, I mean, when you noticed that I was looking at you as I did?"

"An innocent man. The innocence of some child."

Henry reached out for her but she brushed his hand aside.

"And what did such a man seem to be saying to you?" he asked.

"That he loved me with the love of Christ."

Fiona started laughing hysterically.

"How *many* have said *that?* How many indeed?" she remarked with a bitterness that could not be mistaken. "How many have pledged me love and a great deal else if I would sleep with them yet once more? And yet I knew that, most of the time, this would only occur when those blokes were between funds, and had nothing else to give to me but a few warm words and a vague promise or two."

"I meant nothing of the sort," Henry hastened to tell her.

She spun around, a wildness in her eyes.

"I *know!*" she declared, "And that is what upsets me, do you not understand what I am trying to say?"

Fiona breathed deeply.

"No one else has ever looked upon me the way you have."

"How sad. . ." Henry said.

"It *is* sad, mister, I agree with you. But that is the extent of my life."

"We must get out of here now," Cyril interjected, "if any of us is to live at all."

None of them had any idea which way led aboveground.

They knew only one thing: They should go in the opposite direction from which the three Druids had come. So, after taking three torches from holders in the wall, they turned right as soon as they were out of the cavern and walked steadily in that direction.

An hour later, they still had no idea of the proper route to take. But the need to find it was reinforced when they came upon another cavern, and saw that this one was filled with different occupants, those who were not human.

Wooden crates. More than twenty individual crates in all occupied much of the space in that cavern. The contents were not items of food stocked there for a long siege or clothing or medical supplies.

Rats. . . .

Each crate was crammed with a large number of squirming rats, ready to be let out.

The women gasped and shrank back.

"We must eliminate the creatures," Henry stated the obvious.

Cyril could hardly have been in greater agreement.

"Fire," he replied. "We have to destroy them by fire. There is no way I can see that we have, without emerging bitten and bleeding ourselves, and possibly infected, if not with the virus, then with another ailment."

"We should not deplete our torches," Henry offered. "A fresh fire, I think, we should start a fresh fire."

He glanced around and found two suitable rocks.

"I need something to set ablaze," he said as he was about to rub the rocks together. "There is no wood here that I can see except in the crates."

One of the women spoke up.

"My dress," she suggested, anxious to help.

Relieved, Cyril told her that this would be fine, and she tore it apart at the hem, while the others followed her lead.

"Are the men immune?" Fiona asked.

"What do you mean?" Cyril asked.

"Your clothes?"

"My clothes?"

"What are *you* to tear off?"

"Oh, well, I see now. My shirt, and—"

"Your pants."

"I have nothing on underneath. There is too much to explain. Just take my word for it. Our last benefactor had nothing that fit me."

Fiona smiled slyly.

"We can hardly have you walking away naked, can we?"

"The legs," he said, "I will tear off the cloth up to the knees."

"Whatever you say, milord."

A modest pile of ragged patches was now placed in front of the boxes.

"Put it right up against the wood," Henry instructed.

Fiona and Cyril grabbed the pieces and deposited these where he wanted.

"Here goes," Henry told everyone as he brought over the two rocks and sat down next to the little pile.

He failed after three tries. But the fourth was successful. The pieces of cloth ignited in an instant, and Cyril and Henry along with the four women had to step out of the cavern right away because the flames quickly spread to the boxes.

"That sound!" Cyril said. "They are ignorant of what was expected of them, and yet look at how they are being punished."

Holding tight to the torches, they continued down the tunnel, hoping that they did not run into any other surprises except the opening that would lead them aboveground again.

Behind them, rats died. But not all were consumed. Even the survivors, though, were at least slightly burned, and some more than that. All had crossed over into a rodent's version of madness.

And they became a group, a smaller one since so many had perished in the flames, but a group possessed of only one goal: to hunt down those who had been responsible, the scent still strong in their nostrils. But they did not attack right away. Instead they waited, as they followed the six humans who were unaware of them, confident that all of their kind in that cavern had been destroyed. The rats were near-rabid, but able to control themselves as they waited for the right moment, the moment of revenge that consumed every bit of cunning they could muster.

Waiting, ready to attack, looking for an opportunity to pay back what they had suffered, even if they did not, in their dimmed rodent brains, understand the very impulse that drove them ahead, something very close to a common mind uniting them. . . .

CHAPTER 8

More than twenty guards emerged from the tall old trees on three sides of the natural clearing.

Most of the wickerman had burned down to embers and ashes and yet, a small part of it remained standing, the actual altar at the center. On top was a single little body amid piles of bones underneath, bones from other victims that night, that one baby not quite dead.

None of the guards rejoiced as they stood in front of the wickerman and saw the tiny form move, the thin frail arms reaching out briefly into empty air, then pulling back when they touched nothing, a mother not there to hold him, submerging his fear with love that would quickly banish it if given a chance.

"How could it yet live?" Erik Lofton gasped, speaking what every man thought. "How could it have the strength?"

"And for what reason?" Roger Prindiville added. "You know what will have to be done, surely we all do!"

The baby was badly burned. And it cried with the pain of this, very little of its tiny body having escaped the flames.

"He will not live," Prindiville almost whispered. "In that condition he *should not*."

No one could disagree.

"How could even the Druids do this?" John Mottershead asked, stepping away from the wickerman, unable to view the infant any longer.

He turned and walked a few feet from the blackened frame.

"*Oh, my God!*" he wailed, not as a profanity, but a cry of supreme horror and desperation.

The other men spun around.

Prindiville strode forward.

"*What—?*" he said.

Just over a foot from where he was standing was a pit some half-dozen feet deep. Inside were the ravaged bodies of the women who had been sacrificed earlier. And rummaging among them were hundreds of rats, red eyes almost glowing in the darkness not entirely dispelled by the reflected light of an overhead moon.

Prindiville suddenly was very weak and had to lean against Mottershead.

"Is there any hope?" he groaned.

"For Lord Fothergill, Roger?"

"For him? For us? For England, if this has been going on right under our noses, in an age where there are spy devices everywhere, able to scrutinize everything we say, see everything we do?"

Prindiville was not a man who often considered the future but was more content to reminisce, picking from the past moments that he would have been eager to relive.

"If we are to give in to the urgings of our sin nature, no," Mottershead replied. "How *could* hope survive if that were to be so, comrade? Everyone would be doomed, falling in defeat before the coming heathen onslaught."

"Well, I suppose we, men like you and I, Mr. Mottershead, cannot allow this ignominy to raise up, can we, my good man? We cannot let Adam in us triumph. I shall have to hold my vomiting for later, I suspect."

"For when you remember, Mr. Prindiville?"

"Yes, then, Mr. Mottershead, then."

Prindiville stood straight.

"Bring the baby to me," he ordered any of the other knights able to reach into the wickerman without becoming ill.

"I *will* do it," Mottershead volunteered. "Let me take the baby. You have to face your men, knowing that they know what you did, questioning your humanity. I do not. Only Mr. Lofton. The rest of our group is back at Sir Nigel's estate. They need not know. . .ever."

"*I* ordered that the little one be brought to me, not you,

Mr. Mottershead."

The other man protested.

"But you must lead," he said. "Your mind must be clear. How could you think straight so soon after—"

"Should an act of mercy make me less able henceforth? Is that what you are saying? This innocent's agony should be extended, eh?"

"No, but—"

Prindiville had wearied of debate, and left no doubt that he wanted it ended.

"By stabbing a dagger through the heart?" he interrupted purposefully. "Is that how I should do this? What do you say about that?"

Mottershead had been thinking about that.

"No, not that way, Roger. I think you should just hold him. . .you should hold him close to your chest until he stops breathing. He should die in *your* arms against my wishes but permitted by yours, this little one, perhaps causing him somehow to think at last that he is being held by someone who loves him."

"No, it must be by dagger," Prindiville decided finally. "Just holding that frail body would mean pain. Suffocating him would take too long. The suffering *has* to end quickly. That is the only blessing we have to bestow."

Mottershead knew that Prindiville had spoken the truth.

"Forgive me," he acknowledged. "I could not."

"Pray that I can, my brother, pray with all your heart and soul."

He shook his head.

"No more talking. . ." Prindiville grumbled. "I shan't be able to proceed if I am to say one more word."

It was Erik Lofton who stood at the opening in the wickerman. He reached into it and slipped his hands over the wiggling form.

Crying. Not loud. More like anguished little whimpers, all the more pathetic.

The other guards stepped aside and let Lofton pass.

He started crying.

One of the guards nearby whispered, "You are more a man than I, Erik Lofton. You carry the infant. I could not."

Lofton approached Prindiville.

"He could be my son," he said, hesitating. "He could be yours."

"But he is not. His mother's earthly body has become the fodder of those foul creatures in that pit."

"I know what you are saying," Lofton agreed. "It is just so awful, so—"

"The truly awful part is what has been done to him. But that cannot be changed. We must not prolong his agony when the outcome seems as certain as it is. Hand the baby to me without further delay, Mr. Lofton."

"But if any of us allows conscience to be so easily swept aside—"

"Easily, you say? Hardly that, Mr. Lofton."

He thrust his arms forward.

"Enough!" he demanded. "The baby! Now!"

Lofton obeyed.

Prindiville's manner changed as soon as his hands touched that soft, weak form.

"I cannot weaken," he said. "I cannot allow this poor, poor life to be kept from his Creator another moment. *I cannot!*"

A hand on his shoulder.

Prindiville turned slightly to see who it was standing behind him.

"Go on," Mottershead told him. "Go on, my brother. We shall kneel in prayer for you. The Holy Spirit is your companion."

The others must have heard, for the next instant they were on their knees.

"Bless you. . ." Prindiville said as he started toward the wooded area.

After walking a hundred feet or so into it, he saw a pile of leaves.

"Your manger, dear, dear child, oh, God, your manger,"

Prindiville said.

A tiny hand brushed his cheek.

"Do not—" His body shuddered.

For some reason, that hand had not been touched by the flames. It was pink and soft and perfectly formed.

"How could they do this?" he asked. "How could they take a beautiful life before its time and throw it away as though it is mere trash to be burned?"

Weak, racked with pain, the baby could not hold his arm up any longer. As it was falling, Prindiville caught it, and closed his own hand around it.

"And now you will rest in the embrace of the sweet Shepherd Himself," he said softly, tears dripping off his cheeks and onto that helpless, hapless body.

"May I be forgiven this act," Prindiville muttered. "May the angels of heaven not shut the gates at my arrival."

He rested the baby on the bed of autumn-colored leaves. His fingers closed around the handle of a dagger he had owned for more than thirty years, for hunting deer and the like, and withdrew it from its sheath. He looked at the thick blade, sharpened just the day before.

Into Your hands, Heavenly Father, he prayed without speaking.

Then—

"No!" he cried out.

From the center of his soul came a still, small voice, telling him that he must not do what he had persuaded himself to do, that the stench of it would go with him to his grave.

"My Heavenly Father!" he exclaimed, the dagger dropping from his hands.

Driven to his knees, he started weeping in contrition as he said out loud, "Praise Your holy name, my dear Lord. This child is yours. His life is in your hands, not mine."

Roger Prindiville could not do, in the end, what he had resisted the whole of his adulthood, the taking of a life to release the one living it from nearly inconceivable agony, for whatever the name conjured up as camouflage, such an act, stripped of hypocrisy, could be called only what it was, murder.

And so he returned with that tiny, tiny form still breathing, returned to the other men, telling them that doctors would have to judge what hardened modern soldiers could not, the chances for survival of someone so totally dependent on the kindness of strangers. If this sad sweet precious little one were to die before he could be treated, at least the lot of them would have gone the only righteous road they could have traveled.

"We carry him where we must," he declared. "We cannot continue this kind of infamy in the name of mercy."

And every man there, well-seasoned as a result of their profession in witnessing the depravity of others, rejoiced over that, for all had been loath to face their consciences once the baby died by Roger Prindiville's hand. Now they would not have to fight that battle, now they could kneel before God in their prayers without shame.

CHAPTER 9

Elizabeth had had the foresight to pack heavy blankets for her daughters and herself. But she was grateful when the guards started two campfires, the men at one, the women at the other.

She had grown up with fire and found it reassuring. Fireplaces had been built throughout the castle she lived in as a child, and the one to which she moved when she married Cyril Fothergill.

Only once had fire been a source of fear, when the wooded areas so close to the Fothergill castle had gone up in flames. The family was not in any real danger since the exterior portions were of stone and clay, with the only inflammable ones—those made of wood as well as hanging tapestries —safely inside and beyond the reach of any flames, unless embers drifted through any open windows and landed on the exposed wood floors or on the rare Oriental rugs.

"We are so fortunate," she said as she warmed her hands in front of the fire. "Not every family has such truly devoted guards."

She was trying to maintain a thankful stance because, under the circumstances, slipping into self-pity would have been easy, along the lines of, "Why, Lord? Why this? Why have you taken my husband from me, and placed him in such great danger?"

But she generally loathed that sort of thing, considering it a peculiar retreat from reality for a Christian, since *Christ-centered* reality should have made trust automatic, an instinctive reaction to whatever would happen.

But I am human, she thought, *and much weaker than I want to be. Oh, Lord, how I must try Your patience.*

She glanced at the guards.

What a blessing they are, Elizabeth thought, *what good men.*

Her daughters and she had heard stories of the plight of other guards throughout England. "We *are* fortunate," Elizabeth spoke, nodding toward them.

"I know what you mean, Mother," Clarice told her. "Sarah and I have a friend who told us that half their guards are given to drunkenness, and the other half show little or no loyalty. They seem to want only the money."

"And the ease, I imagine," Elizabeth suggested. "None of them really works all that hard, of course. Ours are blessedly quite different. They seem willing to give their lives for us, else they would not be here tonight in the first place."

"Noble. . ." Sarah asserted. "In a curious way they seem noble."

Her mother considered that.

"Noble may be just the right word," she replied. "They also seem content, unless I am being misled."

"I do not think any of them are misleading you," Sarah disagreed, frowning. "But content? I am not so sure, Mother. You may be misunderstanding their behavior. I wonder if resigned may not be more like how they feel. They seem resigned to having no more battlefields to conquer. And they bear this with dignity and nobility."

Elizabeth admitted that her daughter might be right.

"You understand people better than I," she said.

"Me? Are you kidding, Mother?"

"I am not."

"Thank you for saying so, but I am too backward with people ever to understand them as well as you seem to think I do."

"It is wrong to think of yourself more highly than you ought," Clarice objected, "but it is no better to think of yourself as *less* than you are. You have to consider—"

Suddenly both fires were extinguished, but without any wind stirring, not even the feeblest of breezes. And yet not a single glowing ember was left, only a pile of blackened pieces of wood, as if some giant unseen hand had been placed over them, extinguishing them.

The abrupt plunge into darkness and the returning grip of evening frost that had been mostly dissipated by the flames immediately stopped all conversation.

And something else along with this, something that would have chilled them even if the fires were still lit, or it was a humid summer evening.

Howling. . . .

"A dog," Sarah said, "in terrible pain, I think."

She was overwhelmed by how it sounded.

"Should we not look for the poor creature?" she asked.

"Not that, milady," Ladley corrected her.

"Not a dog? It sounds just like—"

He put a finger to his lips and Sarah cut herself off.

And then the agonized howling ceased.

"Over!" Elizabeth said. "Just like that. Gone! What is happening here?"

One of the guards, the newest of those serving the Fothergills, a young man from Northumberland named Oliver Westdyke, jumped to his feet, holding his head.

"So much pain!" he screamed. "My head. . .my head is about to explode. I am unable to stop it from—"

Ladley went to his side.

"We are under attack," he said. "An assault has begun by the *kosmokratoras*. They cannot hurt you if you bar their entry."

"But this is too much," the other man groaned deeply. "How can I ignore the *pain*, Mr. Ladley? It is tearing me apart as I remember, as I—"

"You see something? Is that it, Mr. Westdyke? There is something in your head that is clawing at your brain?"

"So hellish that I—"

"What do you see?" Ladley interrupted.

"Every foul and sinful act I have ever committed!"

Ladley grabbed the man's shoulders.

"We all will join hands now," he said. "They only want to divide us, pick us off one by one. Together we can defeat—"

"*No!*" Westdyke yelled.

He backed away, his eyes wide, as though they would pop from their sockets. In an instant the man had withdrawn an old dagger from his belt and was holding it against his chest.

"There is no hope," he said as he started to sob, "no hope for any of us now or ever. They are too strong. The others for whom we wait are going to be destroyed, cut down like wheat and ground underfoot."

Westdyke grabbed the handle tighter and mumbled, "Forgive me."

"*You shall not do this!*" a voice spoke up powerfully.

Elizabeth was walking toward the man, holding her hands out in front of her.

"Drop the dagger," she ordered. "Drop it and place your hands tightly together."

She did that herself.

"See? Do it, and huddle with me in prayer instead, my good man."

"I am not a good man, milady," the guard told her. "I am a miserable bloke, and you should not sully yourself in my presence."

Her expression was not an unkind one, simply perplexed.

"The demons speak, not your soul," Elizabeth said.

Westdyke could not fathom the way she was treating him. He expected revulsion and contempt, but he saw only compassion.

"But they speak truly," he protested. "They know what I have done. And they will not rest until I am theirs."

"So does the Lord Jesus. And He has already forgiven you."

"He could not forgive what I have done," Westdyke declared. "But even if He does, I am unable to forgive myself."

"What is this sin?" Elizabeth asked. "Tell me, Mr. Westdyke, or I will show you what a *woman's* wrath is all about!"

"Not before my comrades! Not—"

Elizabeth turned and ordered Ladley and the other guards to step back far enough that they could not hear anything.

"Now!" she urged. "Now, no more excuses. . .speak, man, speak before the time to do so has passed. *Do you hear me?*"

"I am a pervert and a murderer," Westdyke said sheepishly. "Look at your face. I see the disgust on it. You think me evil also, more than worthy of a Christless eternity."

Elizabeth's throat went dry, for she had not anticipated anything like that. But freezing a reply in Elizabeth's mouth, however dismayed she was, making her unable to utter anything, was what she saw in the distance.

A shape.

Vague at first but growing more distinct, and with it came sounds, sounds like those of the flapping of leather, and, also, footsteps, but different, like claws across clay tile. . . .

The others saw at the same time what she did, and none of them was less terrorized than Elizabeth.

"Get away from him, Mother!" Clarice shouted.

But Elizabeth stood firm.

Ladley rushed over to her and tried to pull her back.

"How dare you touch me if I do not wish you to do so!" She spoke with the greatest anger she had ever displayed, her words like shards of glass.

"I touch you now for your own good, milady. No other purpose would force me to disobey your command."

She slapped him hard across the cheek.

Ladley fell to his knees.

"I am in disgrace, Lady Fothergill," he muttered.

She ignored him and stared straight ahead at the guard who had not yet plunged the dagger into his chest and, behind him, the outline in the darkness.

"Turn and look!" she demanded. "Turn and look *this very moment!*"

Slowly he turned and saw it, a shape that flickered in and out of visibility. When seen, it filled him with terror. Even the two other guards were unable to speak for fear that its attention would be directed at them.

They now knew, in the center of their souls as well as through what their eyes flashed into their minds, what a creature from hell actually looked like, not the fanciful works of medieval artists or sculptors.

The prince of demons. . . .

And the reality was worse, worse than the most diabolical images anyone could conjure up on canvas or mold into clay.

"This is not merely a demon!" Elizabeth cried out, providentially aware of who the presence was. "We are here with—"

Satan himself, starkly real and standing before them.

The arch deceiver, Elizabeth thought. *But you are not after me, are you? You want my husband. We just happen to be here at the same time. But you shall not have him. Cyril Fothergill is not your property. He belongs to Another.*

Without warning, Elizabeth walked up to Oliver Westdyke, wrenching the dagger from him.

"This is *not* your night of victory," she addressed the presence, holding the weapon in the palm of her hand. "Not one soul among us will be yours."

A great wind swept across the road. Sarah was blown off her feet, taking Clarice with her since they had been tightly holding one another's hand.

"We are not strong, the lot of us!" Elizabeth continued. "But in a tight circle, grasping one another in love and in faith, we *shall* stand up to you, we shall do that very thing!"

Westdyke, no longer with his dagger, shoulders slumping, fell into her arms.

"Milady, milady," he cried, "*help me. . . .*"

She was about to whisper something into his ears when she started gagging.

Odors. . . .

So unspeakably fetid that she could not get her breath, the foul smells invaded her nostrils and quickly went to her lungs.

"I want to live, dear Lord. . ." Elizabeth mumbled weakly. "Please keep me alive to greet my beloved."

Clarice tried to stand and rush to Elizabeth's side, but it

was as though she and her sister had had boulders piled on top of them, not large enough to crush her to death but of such size that they were pinned underneath.

Though yet standing, Ladley and the other guards were no better off, struggling to help but without the strength to do anything but stand and watch and feel the most suffocating shame of their lives.

Like a malignant breeze blowing across an ancient cemetery. . .

The presence moved, and though it seemed to have no physical embodiment, it was able to toss Westdyke to one side.

"Take me," Elizabeth begged of it, "take this soul of mine to damnation forever but spare my dearest love."

A taloned hand reached out for her.

"Lord God, let the blood from Thy only begotten Son on Calvary's cross wash over me and my blessed children and the men here with us," Elizabeth prayed. "Bring to us now the protection of our bodies as well as our souls."

That hand, once shining with a shimmering iridescent beauty among the glories of heaven, but now raw-looking, like beef that had started prematurely to decay, closed around her neck.

Perfect love casteth out fear. . . .

Words read to her during her childhood years by a servant who had had more time for spiritual matters than her mother did.

Perfect love. . .

Her love for her family. Her lifelong love of a Savior Who had seemed ever more real to her as the years passed. And God's love, together with His grace, grace that had brought her through a lifetime brimming over with crisis after crisis.

"No!"

She forced herself to her feet, forced herself to ignore the raging pain of muscles that seemed to be engulfed by a kind of fire searing the inside of her body.

Blood. From her nose.

And a sound. Akin to a gust of wind.

Within it something like laughter arose, but soulless, unutterably cold, the presence before her anticipating what Lady Elizabeth Fothergill would never allow it to have, and ridiculing her determination, knowing that this woman of the aristocracy was mere flesh and blood and, therefore, fallible, subject to falling from grace as were Adam and Eve, and, thus, the stand she was taking, this sudden defiance had to be transitory at most, hardly a challenge of any magnitude, more a pitiable reflex perhaps.

But mere woman that Elizabeth was, she *would* prove the direful presence wrong, for she did know love for and from others, love which the evil one did not comprehend, or know in his own life, such as that life had been for millennia.

"Gather around me, everyone!" Elizabeth told the others. "Place your hand in the grasp of another!"

"We cannot move, milady!" Ladley told her, his voice barely audible.

"You *shall* do *exactly* what I say," Elizabeth commanded the guard who was on her right. "There will be no victory for hell this night."

She moved with an effort so intense that her heart seemed ready to explode, killing her instantly, but she stayed alive nevertheless, placing one foot in front of the other, walking so slowly that, at first, she seemed not to be walking at all.

"But we are weak," Ladley said, trying to dissuade her. "And evil stands strong before us."

Elizabeth's anger blasted out at him.

"Sustained *by* our weakness, driven *by* our fear," she said. "We give him what he needs and he laps it up, like some ravenous dog."

Westdyke was now standing and walking toward her, toward the presence. A moment later, he had placed himself between Elizabeth and the evil one.

"You think nothing but scorn of God's creation," he said, putting his shoulders back, puffing his chest out. "And you want nothing but its destruction."

No reaction. The presence remained motionless. But the guard was no longer allowing himself to be intimidated.

"That shall *not* be what you get," Westdyke continued. "You shall not have even me, the weakest one of those here before you."

He was feeling more and more emboldened.

"Even I, wretch that I have been these years of my life, am beyond your power because I have just accepted Christ Jesus as my Savior, my patient, loving, forgiving Lord, and the Holy Spirit indwells me. My soul is beyond your grasp, now and forever."

Ladley and the other guards had come forward, with Clarice and Sarah. They joined hands, one with the other and repeated a centuries-old chant that was once recited by the early Christians whenever they detected demonic spirits.

"Glory to the Father, and praise to His holy Name, praise to His holy Name, redemption by the death of His Son, redemption by the death of His Son. . .*and all evil vanquished, all evil vanquished.*"

They said this over and over until the presence reared back, like a human being clasping hands over his ears, roaring his frustration to the deaf night air.

Their eyes had been closed as they spoke in prayer.

Light.

They *felt* the brightness before they saw it.

When they opened their eyes, they all were surrounded by it, not some mystical shining with holy crystals at the center or some indeterminate and tepid glow, but a light so bright, so clear, and possessed of such limitlessness that it could have blinded men and women alike. And within that brightness they saw other beings, wholly different from the dark, cold presence, and of such beauty that no one could any longer stand but were forced to their knees on that dirt road, not in fear or weakness but in awe born of seeing and knowing that a part of heaven had descended, infinite stepping into the finite realm.

Oliver Westdyke was weeping.

"I feel so clean," the words burst out of his mouth. "How can I feel so clean, having done what I have done, having wallowed in the gutter of my depraved nature?"

"Because there are more than angels here," Elizabeth said, her voice husky. "They have been sent as heralds but He has followed them, and we stand in *His* presence, that *other* vanquished."

"Just as we prayed," Westdyke conceded.

And they looked up into a Face, for an instant only, a Face so good, fine, pure, and loving, a Face so kind and holy, a single glimpse was sufficient to push all of them forward on the ground as each gasped from the sublime glory of their majestic encounter, kneeling no longer an adequate response, but only absolute contrition suitable, their lips touching the dirt, tasting of it, mixed as it was with the salt of their tears.

CHAPTER 10

Waiting, ready to attack, looking for an opportunity to get even for what they had suffered, even if they did not, in their dimmed rodent brains, understand the very impulse that drove them ahead, something very close to a common mind uniting them. . . .

The attack by the rats would come in a short while but not before Cyril, Henry, and the four remaining women came upon a cavern with a low ceiling and a funnel-shaped opening in it that led to the surface. From a miniature underground lake of boiling water steam arose through the opening.

"The ground in one corner of the clearing always had a curious characteristic, from what I have heard," Cyril told the others. "It seemed warm to the touch, and every so often, when there was little rain and the soil was dry and cracked, some of that steam would escape into the air. At night, with the moonlight on it, this gave rise to all sorts of ghost tales.

"Those who had seen this once thought it might signal the beginnings of volcanic activity of some sort. And others, especially the superstitious poor of this region, wondered if perhaps there was not some connection with the location of hell."

. . .some connection with the location of hell.

That possibility made him pause, while thinking that, back in the catacombs, he had been as close to hell as he ever wanted to come.

"Then it happened that a small portion of ground caved in just after the turn of the century," he went on. "Seeing geysers of steam shoot up, levelheaded people then came to understand that this was just a natural phenomenon."

He breathed in deeply.

"Strange. . . ." he said.

The water had an odd smell to it.

"Eggs. . ." Henry ventured, testing it as well. "I wonder if it is not like the odor of boiling eggs."

"Interpretation of smell is in the nose of the beholder," Cyril joked. "But I think it seems more like some kind of mineral that is being cooked by the heat from below and as it filters into the water, it sends up what you and I detect now."

One of the women who had been standing next to the tunnel screamed.

"Eyes!" she cried, terrified. "Little red eyes were staring at me."

The others reacted nervously, moving closer to one another and mumbling.

Cyril tried to calm them down.

"A few rats might have escaped the fire," he said. "But certainly not enough to be worried about."

"More than a few," the woman insisted. "I saw *many* pairs, Lord Fothergill. As soon as I called out, they disappeared."

The experience Cyril had in the catacombs under St. Peter's was not forgotten.

"I know how you feel," he told her.

"How *could* you know? You probably think I am nothing more than a crazy woman."

"I do not think that at all. But I *do* know how you must have felt when you saw them, demonic little eyes as though they were peering at you from the outer reaches of hell itself, waiting for the moment when they would spring."

The woman's eyes widened.

Cyril saw her reaction, and decided to tell them all, in truncated form, that he had undergone a short while before.

The four women became emotional as he spoke, their faces either frozen with shock or foreheads wrinkled, biting their lower lips, eyes half-closed as they reeled from the images he created.

After Cyril had finished, the woman who had inadvertently forced him to recall his experiences said, "Forgive me, milord. I had no idea. Forgive my impertinence."

"But you were not altogether wrong, I suppose," he said. "Except I walk in your shoes, I cannot know *exactly* the feelings you had.

"I still condemn what you have done with your lives," Cyril added, "but we all are weak again and again, or we would not give in to our sin natures. If we were *always* strong enough to fend off the enemy of our souls, he would never gain a victory."

The heat from the bubbling little underground lake had a restorative effect on everyone. But they knew that they could not stay much longer, for there was no way of knowing where the Druids were or if they were in pursuit.

Henry heard some movement out in the tunnel, muted sounds that might not have been heard at all except by chance.

"Look!" he yapped, jumping to one side.

Scores of pairs of crimson-red eyes were puncturing the darkness.

Henry held his torch out in front of them.

The forms of more than a hundred rats could be seen before they ran to his left partway down the tunnel. Then they stopped, stopped abruptly at the feet of someone who was standing in the middle, a hooded figure, motionless, unspeaking.

"The high priest!" Cyril exclaimed after Henry had motioned him over.

"But how do you know that?" Henry asked.

"That crescent on his hood."

The only surviving Druid of that group was surrounded by the only surviving rats, most of them standing on their hind legs and looking up at him.

Waiting. . . .

The little creatures were waiting, or so it seemed, waiting for his command, the fur of most of them singed, some with feet badly burned, quite a few with part of their tails missing, the flesh on their backs trembling.

"Excited, I think," Cyril said. "They seem—"

He was starting to sweat, not so much from the steam of

that place, the hot water bubbling out from within the earth but rather, from wondering if he would be trapped again, in another tunnel, by another group of rats controlled by another master.

"You have mentioned more than once this Gervasio," he could hear Henry recalling, the torch shaking a bit as the other man shuddered. "Was he not able to control rats?"

Cyril nodded, sorry that the name had been spoken again.

"Could Gervasio have come to England before you returned?" Henry asked.

Cyril had not seriously regarded that possibility before, but now he was forced to do so.

"He probably could, Henry. Posing as a Druid might well be something Baldasarre Gervasio would find appealing."

"Then he could be yonder high priest whose identity we cannot make out."

Cyril saw where the other man was heading, and shook his head.

"I am sure this one is not the Gervasio I encountered," he said.

"But why?" Henry asked. "It would be logical—"

"The man who tried to kill me was shorter and thinner, not much over a hundred pounds perhaps," Cyril said. "This one is rather tall, broad-shouldered. Believe me when I say that there is no comparison between them."

The hooded figure stood, whispering briefly, then silent, his features hidden.

"What is he waiting for?" Cyril asked out loud. "He seems to be studying us. What is he trying to find out?"

Glancing at him curiously, Henry said with marked apprehension, "There is something more than that."

"What more could there be?"

"He uttered your name."

"My name? How could he possibly know who I am?"

"He might have overheard one of the women earlier."

Cyril sensed that Henry was not telling him everything and asked, "Is that it? Or do you have anything else to tell me?"

Henry, nodding, said. "I thought I heard him do that just a moment ago, no more than a whisper but quite clear."

"But I would have noticed as well."

"Not talking, Cyril. He seemed to be forcing back a sob."

Cyril found that very difficult to accept, assuming that Henry had simply misunderstood whatever the sound was.

"A sob?" he questioned. "How could you have heard that?"

"At sea you learn to be as alert as you can, to the presence of gulls, for example, because they indicate that land is nearby or there are a hundred other sounds that are important. My hearing is strong, Cyril, always has been, and my intuition stronger yet."

Something happened then for which there would be but a partial explanation only later, given when Elizabeth and her daughters and the guards left behind to protect them could tell Cyril, Henry, and the women of the encounter they were having at precisely that instant aboveground.

The rock floor under them shook, the rock walls of the tunnel lit by light so intense that it seemed as though the sun itself had broken with time and space, and invaded that underground region with brilliance upon which no one could look for long.

The Druid shrank from it, bending over nearly double, his hood almost falling back.

Now I will see who you are, Cyril thought, *sucking in his breath. You will no longer be able to hide. I shall have all of England hunt you down if you manage to escape.*

But the high priest grabbed the hood in time and kept it over his head.

In the meantime, the women could neither fall to the ground nor run from that place. Instead they bowed their heads and stretched their hands outward, palms up.

"*Father, forgive us our sins!*" Fiona cried out for them all.

The two men joined them.

"Take my hand!" Cyril called to the others as he reached for Henry to his left, and the women to his right.

"We are so unworthy, defiled, weak," one woman began, hesitating in her long-held shame.

"His strength is made perfect in our weakness," Cyril told her. *"Take my hand now! Join with the rest of us!"*

He began to repeat the Lord's Prayer, and their voices blended with his and Henry's.

A purging at Woodhenge. . . .

Evil faced the light of heaven and began to scamper away but not without a last stand, not before the cleansing was forestalled in a dying surge of grasping malevolence.

Despite the glow, despite a sound that seemed like some distant choir capable of the most sublime musical beauty, the high priest, in the end, would not relent. Instead he opened his arms before the rats and seemed about to issue a command, a command that would propel them to carnage that he would not forestall any longer. It would be his final offering to the invisible but hovering prince of darkness.

No words.

His throat was paralyzed. Only incomprehensible gurgling sounds escaped his lips.

He shook his fists at the light.

And it was gone.

The Druid laughed as he straightened up, his defiance returning.

"My master's power is stronger, Lord God Jehovah," he shouted. "Someday I shall see *You* in hell!"

Cyril stepped forward. Only a few feet separated them.

"You speak blasphemy!" he rebuked the other man.

"If you are right, it only shows further how weak the so-called Almighty Creator of heaven and earth is. Almighty? How laughable. I shook my fists and the light vanished."

He spat on the ground at Cyril's feet.

"If He ever showed Himself, I would spit in His face as well. No, I would do more than that. I would—"

Suddenly the Druid high priest gasped and staggered

forward a few inches, then spun around.

Eyes wide with the satisfaction that only a man of experience battling criminals feels, Roger Prindiville stood squarely in the middle of the tunnel, his fingers wrapped around the black marble handle of an ancient dagger, its blade dripping blood.

"You are not to condemn any more helpless women!" Prindiville declared. "The gates of heaven are closed to you and your kind forever."

He raised the dagger a second time.

"Your kind were once banished from Britain for their shameful practices. *So shall it be again!*"

The guard thrust the dagger one more time into the Druid, but missed his heart, the blade entering his shoulder instead, and he fell back against the rock wall of the tunnel, mumbling something that sounded like an incantation.

The rats reacted, all of them scrambling in Prindiville's direction.

Why not after us? Cyril wondered from a dozen feet away. *Are we, for some reason, to be allowed escape? Why the reluctance to—?*

Then the hooded figure let out a cry that could not have been more terrifying if it had come from Satan himself. And the rats sprang forward, leaping onto Prindiville, as well as the knights directly behind him.

"*Go!*" Cyril said to Henry and the women.

They started running, but Cyril, oddly, hesitated.

Why do I not hasten after the others? he thought. *What is it about this Druid that keeps me here?*

He faced the high priest, now shorn of any terror his image might have cast moments earlier, wounded, not able to stand straight but leaning against the tunnel wall.

"You are surely dying. . ." he said. "Let me talk to you of Christ Jesus, Son of the living God. Let me tell you of redemption for eternity before it is too late."

Groaning from his wound, the hooded figure stumbled toward Cyril, a trail of blood from his back down to the floor of the tunnel behind him.

"Who are you?" Cyril asked as he backed into the steam-shrouded cavern.

The high priest reached out his arms, almost in a supplicatory gesture.

"I regret so much, dear Cyril, that all this could not have worked out differently," the voice lamented. "I would have liked to have gone from here to live a satisfying life and be content even in a troubled world while you lived that way as well, and perhaps, for the two of us to grow old together. But now, cruelly, you and I are doomed."

He brushed Cyril's cheek with his fingers.

"I could have loved you. . ." he whispered.

And then his hands closed around Cyril's neck.

"You are so intelligent, yet such a fool!" the Druid growled. "There is no epidemic. It is only an elaborate hoax to torment—"

They struggled near the edge of the underground lake. Without the dagger wound, the high priest would have possessed sufficient strength to be the victor but he was too weak by then, and Cyril managed to break away, sending him sprawling on the ground, where he remained for a moment, before getting to his feet unsteadily.

"Who is behind all this?" Cyril demanded. "Who dreamed up such a hoax, as you claim it is? And why? What pleasure have you and the others gotten out of conjuring a nightmare with millions as its victims? I demand to know—"

The other man had grabbed a small rock and was concealing it in his right hand.

"Too late!" he interrupted. "There are no more answers because the questions have become so meaningless."

He swung the rock, struck Cyril on the temple, and raised it to hit him again as he started to fall. For a moment, the high priest froze, seeing the pain on Cyril's face, hearing him groan, and looking, in that instant, at the man's helplessness, which made him unable to fend off any final, fatal blow.

The Druid let out a cry quite different from the earlier

one, a cry of despair and frustration that shook his entire body.

"*I cannot do this,*" he muttered, his throat obviously sore, and dropped the rock, then stood at the edge of the underground lake.

He looked at his hands with contempt.

"Babies, Cyril, *babies!*" he said, sobbing. "I see their blood on these hands of mine, deep unholy pools of it soaking both, and I am unable to abide this any longer. I have hungered to be free before now, you know, to be cleansed but that has never happened."

He dropped his hands at his sides.

"No man could endure this," he went on, "the shame, the condemnation within my very soul, but it does not end there. . .something else, something altogether different, something that consumes me even now, *especially* now, sinful desires that twist my very soul—"

The Druid glanced back at Cyril as he threw off the hood at last.

"—the longing, the nightly longing that nothing could satisfy, nothing except—"

He cut himself off, but smiled as he added, in a whisper, "Good-bye, my dear Cyril, good-bye. Where I go, you cannot be. . .even if I desired it so."

The Druid high priest staggered briefly, his last bit of strength gone, and then, screaming, tumbled into the red-hot water, disappearing down into the depths of that boiling lake, long thought as it was by the ignorant poor farm folk of that region during medieval times and later to be the gateway to hell.

For Lord Geoffrey Cowlishaw, ten thousand shrieking demons proclaimed ancient peasants wise.

CHAPTER 11

Cyril Fothergill was unconscious when the guards brought him, Henry, and the four women out of the underground tunnel system. His wife and daughter were at his side during the trip back to the family castle. As Elizabeth had anticipated the need for medical help, there were two physicians waiting when they arrived who expressed dismay upon seeing both men. Despite their respite as Nigel Selwyn's guests, the men were undernourished and dehydrated, and it seemed that every muscle in their bodies had been misused for they were filled with aches and pains.

But it was more than their physical selves that needed healing. For Henry, it meant that his desire to return to France had to be delayed significantly. He was not well enough to endure the rigors of another long and possibly dangerous trip back the way he had come, especially across the English Channel where bad weather would dominate for many more weeks.

But it was Cyril who had suffered more greatly. It was Cyril for whom the process of recovery would take a very long time. Prime Minister Edling was sensitive to this, suspecting at least some of what the other man had been forced to endure, and left him alone for a day or two before calling both to find out how he was getting along, and to learn the details of what had happened. . . .

A week later, Cyril was standing in the middle of the family rose garden when Elizabeth came from the castle to tell him that lunch soon would be ready.

"These bushes and the arbors have been here for generations," he mused. "Nothing seems to destroy them, not pests, not the bitter winters, or the heat of summer. There have been times when they were endangered but they survived, and they grew beautiful again."

Cyril had sat down on an old wooden stool, not very comfortable, and yet when Elizabeth offered to have something better brought out from the castle, he told her that this was not needed.

"If it were a bed of nails," he said, sighing, "it would seem just fine because I am here with my loved ones and away from—"

She saw that his left hand was shaking and so she sat on the grass at his feet, holding that hand in her own.

"You need say nothing," she told him, "now, ever."

"But saying something *is* what I need," he replied.

"Then go ahead, my love. Say what you want, for however long you need, and I shall listen to every word as never before."

He leaned over and kissed her on the forehead.

"You do not take me seriously?"

"I take you very seriously. But you seem so solemn just now. Please smile for me. I need to see your face light up."

He tried but could not.

"They took your joy," Elizabeth said. "They took it and sacrificed it on their unholy altar."

"It was gone before I fell captive to the Druids."

"Tell me everything, will you, dear? You said you needed to talk. I need to hear what you say. While you were gone, I awoke night after night, thinking that you had returned, and there you were, in the darkness, ready to surprise me. But I realized that it was only a lonely woman's fantasy."

He told her some of it. He told her of the ratman, of the remains of the apostle Peter, of—

"Hold me tighter," he pleaded as he slid off the stool and joined her on the ground. "Hold me, if you can, until my bones threaten to break. I shall not mind because it is you, and your sweetness is a comfort to me."

She hugged him with all her strength.

"There were rats," he muttered.

"Did that Gervasio send them after you?" Elizabeth asked.

"Yes, he did. I almost died there. I still imagine that they are all over me, their strange musky odor clogging my nostrils."

"And Pope Adolfo? Was he a good man?"

"I think he was, is. I think he wants to do the right thing, but his vision is clouded by men such as Gervasio who realize his utter dependency upon them."

"You said yesterday that the epidemic was a hoax."

He was silent as he rested his head on her shoulder.

"But you are not so sure?" she asked, knowing her husband's manner well.

"It may be, yes, it may be."

"And how cruel if that is so, but then, should you not feel relieved?"

"If Edling becomes convinced that it is nothing more than that, he will let down his guard. And he will never allow me to see him again if that is what I want to discuss."

"But if the threat were a farce, then you should not concern yourself whatever his outlook."

She rubbed a hand across his cheek.

"There is nothing more to be done," she said. "If the whole world turns its back on you in this matter, how could you go on? You would be like Jeremiah but without the victory he experienced."

"Elizabeth?" he asked, and she could see his reluctance.

"No one else is around," she told him. "We are alone. You can tell me whatever you want. If it is making love to me right now, out here, then we shall do that."

"There was someone."

She sucked in her breath, sorry that she had introduced the subject and given him an opportunity to speak of it.

"A woman?" she asked.

"No. . . ."

"Then who?" Elizabeth probed, not pleased by his reticence but trusting her husband regardless of it.

"Geoffrey Cowlishaw."

"The man Edling sent along with you."

"Yes."

"Was he not what you expected?"

He said nothing, though he chuckled a bit to himself at the understatement of what Elizabeth had just said.

"What do you want to tell me about this man?"

"I think—" he started to say, his hand trembling all the more.

"We will do this another day," she assured him.

"Not another day. Not another minute. It has to be now. I have to tell you about Geoffrey."

She saw that he was crying.

"I will listen," she said. "Whatever you have to tell me, I *will* listen."

"I liked him very much," Cyril said. "I have so few friends. I am not a man who gathers them around himself, you know."

"But you are less frivolous than many I could mention. And a fine Christian. Because you eschew debauchery, many men find you dull."

"Geoffrey did not, Elizabeth. Geoffrey found me—"

He stopped again.

Before Cyril could continue, Elizabeth dried his tears with a linen handkerchief, a pretty little piece of cloth that Sarah had embroidered for her the year before.

"He seemed like a brother," he went on. "And I accepted him as such. We laughed, we cried, especially about those whales I told you about yesterday. We found so much that we could agree on. And our experiences were part of a bonding that I thought would last now and through eternity."

Elizabeth was beginning to sense what her husband wanted to tell her but she kept her peace.

"When it seemed that rats had been sent to murder him, I almost gave up," he recalled. "The evil of which men are capable! We have seen glimmers of it from time to time but in that revelation about Geoffrey, I felt as though hell had been opened up and I was staring down its horrible maw!"

"He seemed a new but dear friend. You were told some monstrous details about his death. You should not be ashamed of your reaction."

"But when we confronted one another in the caverns, just before Prindiville and the others managed to kill those rats—"

She could feel the sobs welling up inside him.

"We can stay here as long as you want. The staff need not know. Clarice and Sarah need not know either. Cry as much as you want, my dearest."

"You cannot know why."

"But I do, I know what you are feeling. You are not alone in this way, far from it, Cyril. Look at me now, will you?"

He raised himself up and looked into her wise eyes.

"Am I still beautiful?" she asked.

"Very beautiful. You have never been less than beautiful."

"It does not shock you that men are still attracted to me."

"But no man *dare* touch you!"

"No man has."

The tears were stopping. Elizabeth knew her man, and how to reach into his very soul. It was not all that she had learned over the years but it was of the greatest importance, at other times as well as that, when he felt in despair, and though God had not rejected him, God was not speaking, and she needed to do so instead.

Elizabeth spoke slowly.

"No man dare touch me, as you say, but there have been women who have tried."

Cyril tumbled over on his back.

And Elizabeth burst out laughing.

"It was hardly *that* funny!" he exclaimed.

"Oh, it was, beloved, trust me, it was."

He righted himself and insisted upon knowing who they were.

"The wives of lords who were abominable to them. I showed each some sympathy, and they thought it was something more."

. . .they thought it was something more.

"Geoffrey must have been like that," Cyril admitted.

"And you probably are wondering what you did to encourage him," she said without hesitating, without letting him know how startled she really was.

"*Encourage* him? Nothing! How could I be that stupid, Elizabeth?"

"If you love another human being, is that stupid, my husband?"

"I did not love—"

Her eyes widened.

"Be very sure of what you say," Elizabeth advised. "Love is not wrong. Love is pure. I love you. You love me. Our daughters love *us*, Cyril. Can there be anything wrong in one man *correctly* loving another?"

"But he thought—"

"That was his sin, do you not see that? It was not yours. You loved him as a friend. But Geoffrey wanted more."

"He spared my life."

"As you would have spared his."

"And yet the man is in hell."

"Where he deserves to be."

He threw his head back and tried to scream but no sound came from his mouth, and there were no more tears, as though he had been drained of them.

Elizabeth held his head between her hands.

"He murdered women. He murdered babies. He murdered others, we can be sure."

"But he let me live."

"Cherish that. Do not question it. God uses any vessel He chooses, no matter how broken, no matter how dirty."

Noticing that she was starting to shiver, he said, "We should go in now."

As they both stood, he told her, "Go ahead, I will follow you in a minute or two."

She kissed him on the cheek.

"You wonder why there could have been love, any kind

of love, from Geoffrey Cowlishaw or anyone else. You still think of yourself as a cold, unlovable man."

"I do, oh, Elizabeth, I do. Will I ever be free of that?"

She simply smiled knowingly at him, then turned and walked slowly back to the castle.

"The west wall, Elizabeth," he called to her. "I shall be there briefly, and then it is time for lunch. Tell the girls to be patient."

"They know you," she said, raising her voice, "and if you are at lunch when the food is piping hot or when it is stone cold they will hardly stop loving you. Follow your heart, Cyril. The Holy Spirit will handle the rest."

At the west wall he could view a stretch of land that was flat except for trees and the outlines of other castles even though an early afternoon mist kept out most of the sun's rays that day.

"My England!" he exclaimed out loud. "You may be safe after all."

Cyril then stretched his hands out before him in a vaguely pontifical gesture. "How much I love you, how much I love your people, the soil of your fields, the distant moors, your castles and streams, your past, your present—"

He did not want more tears. He fought them, fought them hard, and they would not come, so strong was his determination.

"—and your future, now I know that you will not be destroyed by what madmen plan. How many more generations will live and die on these ancient isles, my beloved England? King Arthur himself must be rejoicing as he bows before the God of heaven and earth. I say, as he must, I say, 'Long live this land of kings and Christendom. May its glory shine through the ages of time to come, this England, this immortal land of my birth, the land I love that no longer may be threatened by pestilence.' "

He found himself kneeling, and now he stood.

"I owe you that, Geoffrey," he whispered. "I owe you the

truth if that be it. Which is something, is it not?"

As he went inside the castle to rejoin his loved ones, a tear slipped down his rugged cheek, but only one.

Geoffrey Cowlishaw received no more.

CHAPTER 12

"You seem so tired now," Elizabeth told him, putting into words what had concerned her since his return.

"I am," Cyril replied. "I have been hit at so many different levels of my life. I wish I could pluck out of my brain what I have seen, what I have heard, but it all remains lodged there, like some terrible octopus with its tentacles reaching out to every corner, groping its way into—"

Elizabeth frowned. "Go upstairs, please. Get some rest. Sleep through until dinner if you like."

"I would like that very much but I have no idea if I can just doze off. I have not been able to do so for some time. How I long for the days when sleep comes easily, and my dreams are pleasant ones, not filled with the horrors that I have experienced."

"If you cannot, you give *them* a victory, you know."

"A victory, Elizabeth?"

"You tell the enemy that their hold on you has not been broken, that the reach of this little ratman and whoever his accomplices might be, human and demonic, is more far-reaching and stronger than your ability, with God's help, to turn your back on it. They *control* you as a result, Cyril. Is that what you want?"

"Of course not!" he protested, annoyed that his wife would even raise the issue.

"Then go to bed, close your eyes, and let the angels guard you round about."

He smiled as she said that, for belief in angels was mushrooming, evidenced in all the arts and in conversations at every social level.

"That should be quite enough," he told her, hoping that she was right. "How foolish I must seem."

"No more so than any other man caught in the nightmare

that surrounded you."

"But Henry seems to be taking it less grievously than I."

And that was true of this man whose mind was supposedly impaired. He had the knack of getting through something that may have been devastating at the time but, after a while, he just released its memory, and went on about his life, largely as though the nightmare had never happened in the first place.

"Henry is a dear man, a sweet man, surely every bit this, yet the limitations of his mind are hardly unnoticeable."

"But I suppose that they are a blessing right now. After all, he shared many of the experiences with me."

"Do not suppose, my husband. *Know* that his *limitations* are a blessing to this man. With added ability comes added *responsibility* and, be very certain about this, increased attacks from the enemy of our souls."

"You sound like someone who should be speaking from a pulpit."

"Find a church in England that would allow me to do so and I shall rise to the occasion, my beloved."

They had been standing at the bottom of the staircase leading to the living quarters floor of the castle. Cyril looked up the steps at the doorway to their bedroom.

"It would be nice to be with you now," he whispered.

"But you must have your rest. I want you full of vigor and passion."

"I hope I can please you when we are together."

"Have you *forgotten* how?"

"Not at all," he told her, wincing.

"After all these weeks, I am counting on it!" she declared, winking at him.

They kissed and then he started up the stairs.

"Will you hold me, dear, dear Elizabeth, just for a moment?" he asked.

She joined him on the fifth step and they embraced, the warmth of her body against his making him regret his need to sleep just then.

"I will never leave you again," he promised.

"Nor I, now or for eternity."

She watched him walk up the remaining steps and enter their bedroom, shutting the door behind him.

Dear Lord, thank You for bringing that man home to me, she prayed. *I doubt that I could have gone on without him.*

She heard footsteps on the bare wooden floor behind her. Clarice and Sarah.

"Is everything all right, Mother?" Clarice asked for both of them.

"It is," Elizabeth replied, "praise the name of Jesus, it truly, truly is!"

Cyril slept until dusk.

He was awakened by Clarice who was sitting on the edge of his bed as she tapped him gently on the shoulder.

"Dinner is going to be on the table soon, Father," she said.

"Dinner? Have I been asleep as long as that?"

"All of the afternoon."

A slight grimace crossed his face.

"Your mother must be annoyed with me," he remarked.

"Why would she?" Clarice asked, feigning ignorance.

"She probably wanted to spend some time with me before we ate, and here I am, paying no attention to her."

"Mother understands, I have no doubt about that."

"I hope so. I shall get ready now. Thank you for awakening me."

Clarice nodded, a curious look about her.

"Is there anything wrong?" he asked.

"Nothing, Father, there is nothing wrong."

Still, he was uncertain. After she left, he found himself wondering if bad news awaited him when he finally made it downstairs.

Clarice did not seem upset, he thought. *And yet I am sure she was hiding something.*

He washed, changed his clothes, and started to open the door but hesitated, bowing his head in prayer, hoping that he had imagined whatever it was he saw in daughter—the way she held her head, her tone of voice, whatever else it was—that set off an alarm in him.

Cyril walked cautiously out into the hallway, his strength yet subpart, and approached the steps leading downstairs.

The first floor at that location was one huge open room.

He took the steps carefully, feeling a little weak but not particularly unsteady, and looked from one end to the other.

Empty.

It was completely empty, with only a few chairs pressed up against each wall. When the guest list for a particularly large banquet was being planned, Elizabeth would have an extra table moved into this room so, in effect, there was a third dining hall at their disposal to handle any overflow.

No one.

As Cyril reached that first floor, he looked at the family portraits hanging from each wall, tracing their way back over previous generations, his father, his grandfather, his great-grandfather, and others. An innate appreciation of antiquity and heritage never waned.

I could imagine a form of hell being some place where there was no sense of ancestry, where traditions just did not exist, he thought, shivering as he did so.

A door in the east wall was suddenly opened by a member of the household staff, and the Fothergill family guards entered, led by Roger Prindiville.

After they had formed a line, the door in the north wall was opened as well, as though according to a well-rehearsed plan. This time, it was Elizabeth, followed by Clarice and Sarah and the two Selwyn knights, Erik Lofton and John Mottershead, followed by members of the household staff who were not busily involved preparing the evening meal.

Next, the door in the west wall was swung open, and the four prostitutes entered, each now thoroughly bathed and expertly coiffured as well as brightly dressed, all of them looking almost serene. Following them were a number of the other lords of that region.

Lord Alfred Hatterley stood before Cyril.

"I have agreed to support the four women whose lives you saved," he said. "They will join my household staff and their children will be given the proper schooling. They will never have to worry about the bills of physicians or any other expenses, certainly not clothes, food, and the like. I shall also try to find them husbands!"

Everyone in the room broke out into applause.

Cyril put his arms around the other man.

"God bless you, Alfred," he whispered.

"He is doing that at this very moment."

Hatterley returned to his position among the others.

Another door in another wall, the remaining one, was still closed.

A minute or two passed.

The door remained shut.

Then it was opened slowly. And a single figure stepped through, while many others hovered behind him.

Prime Minister Harold Edling.

He bowed before Cyril, who was stunned.

"Before you, I am but a nondescript footnote in some historian's journal," Edling declared. "Those scribes like men who stand up for their rights and the rights of other Englishmen, they like men who are willing to lose their lives for their country and their countrymen. I am not certain I can ever measure up."

Now upright, Edling smiled at Cyril.

"The mission I gave you was performed with valor," he said.

Cyril felt uncomfortable receiving any praise. His relief and joy at returning home obscured the fact that he felt he accomplished nothing. And if the hantavirus plot had been real, he could have blamed himself for the deaths of millions of people.

"But I was not successful," he protested politely. "In fact, I failed quite miserably."

Edling would not let him settle into such a rut.

"Would your death have been penance for any such failure?" he asked with an edge of scorn to his voice. "I do not accept that nor can I believe that the Creator imposes it."

Cyril forced himself to avoid blurting out any truths which some others in the room might not know. While aware that the secrecy regarding his trip had been shattered, he sensed that the fewer specifics that were revealed, the better Edling would feel.

And yet he obviously misread the situation.

Edling motioned for someone else to come into the room.

A round-faced, overweight, but well-dressed Frenchman named Louis Lafontant, dispatched by the president of France, entered with a flourish.

"My dear friends in Paris are less skeptical than I initially was," Edling said.

Lafontant stepped forward.

"We are quite ready to join with the British in mounting another crusade if necessary, after all these hundreds of years," he said with an aristocratic arrogance. "Those wild, uncivilized creatures must be taught a lesson this time."

The sounds of people gasping echoed through the room.

Hatterley spoke up, alarmed. "Another *crusade?*"

He was sputtering as he repeated those two words.

"What could possibly be the justification for this?"

Edling indicated Cyril with a wave of his hand.

"It is a story to tell that would be best told by a man who has lived so much of it," he said, smiling proudly. "Why do we not all sit down, have a wonderful meal, and then listen to what Lord Fothergill has to say?"

Lafontant strode up to Cyril and shook his hand.

"You are a hero in my country," he said.

"Before tonight, I was feeling like a fool in mine."

"Very admirable, sir, this Christian humility. But I must say that, right now, you stand on the world stage as someone whom armies would follow to the place of the damned if that were where you chose to lead them."

. . .*to the place of the damned.*

"It seems almost that I have been there, monsieur, but I was alone at the time, no armies to help."

"You will have nation after nation serving you this time, Lord Fothergill. Your Richard the Lion Hearted will no longer take center stage and command all the attention, even posthumously, I assure you."

"I am sorry to disappoint you, but there is going to be no—" Cyril started to say.

Edling immediately interrupted him.

"You are still so tired," he said. "I can tell by looking at you. Why not cease further discussion, even with our distinguished visitor, and begin the banquet that has been prepared in your honor? Afterward, if you feel revived, you can spin some true tales for us."

He turned to Lafontant.

"Please, my dear Louis," he added, "go with the others and take your seat now. I need to speak with Lord Fothergill in private a moment."

The Frenchman acquiesced politely.

Cyril and Edling walked to the eastern door while a member of the prime minister's staff quickly opened it for the two of them. They stepped into a small hallway that connected to the vestibule.

"You must not tell anyone that the plot may be nothing more than an elaborate charade," Edling told him as soon as they were completely alone.

"But that is probably what it will turn out to be," Cyril protested.

"Or it may not and the epidemic will be upon us after all. Can we afford to let down our guard?"

Cyril knew Edling well enough to realize that the man was keeping something from him.

"Is there more to this?" he asked.

Edling, normally someone able to look another man straight on, and without blinking, seemed then a bit shiftier.

"Why do you ask that?" he asked.

"You once told me that I had insights into human nature

that seemed beyond most men."

"Yes, I did, Cyril. But get to the point, please."

"You yourself no longer believe that this plot is anything more than a cruel practical joke offered by the enemy."

"I suspect the enemy of a great deal. I do not believe we will ever be free of his conniving. He beat us on the battlefield but that is not enough. Anything else he can do to unsettle us, he *will* do."

"But is not panic over the possibility of an epidemic what they plan rather than the outbreak itself?"

Edling saw that pretense was useless.

"I think *that* is precisely it," he acknowledged.

Cyril was becoming confused, and not a little alarmed.

"But you stopped me from telling Lafontant."

Edling was uncomfortable because he knew Cyril to be a man of morality and ethics to an uncommonly high degree.

"The Germans are coming around. . .so are the Italians."

"You got through to Adolfo?" he asked.

"I did, and he is now much closer to our point of view. Nor is he the only one."

"But if there is no plot against us, what will happen to this unusual harmony, given that it is built upon a foundation of the most catastrophic need?"

"It can be nurtured a hundred ways, Cyril. There is no paucity of combinations. Harmony can lead to alliances, you know."

"Harmony can lead to alliances, yes, of course," Cyril agreed, repeating those words.

"You are not a politician, Cyril. I am, as is Adolfo, and so are they who—"

He saw Cyril's expression.

"Are you beginning to understand now?" Edling asked.

"I am. The threat of the epidemic has brought you and other elected leaders together. There are political advantages to this, especially if the opposition now thinks twice about trying to 'dethrone' a leader whose influence has grown overnight."

The next part was what upset him.

"But if there is no epidemic, all that could go up in smoke, laying waste to the machinations of statespersons and scoundrels."

Assuming that he was not being counted among the latter group, Edling nodded in complete agreement.

"That is why there must be nothing done to speed up awareness of this Muslim charade. It will come in time, anyway, of course it will. I see the inevitability as much as you apparently do, my dear Cyril, but by then treaties will have been signed, military pacts finalized, and economic cooperation brought into being, and all functioning so flawlessly that such would never be abandoned."

"After seeing the demonstrable benefits of all this, not even the absence of those conditions that brought everything into being will be enough to break up what you have wrought."

"Is not the human mind most extraordinary, Cyril?"

"What about the human heart, Harold? And what about the soul?"

The prime minister was uncomprehending.

"What about those people who will live in the worst sort of fear until their governments announce the truth to them? What about those who would be driven into perverse avenues of experience, thinking that to eat, drink, and be merry is all that is left to them? And the others, the weak, no longer able to endure the threat, who would turn to suicide as a result?"

"There has always been debauchery. And at times it seems the weak are the ones who will inherit the earth. But they would contribute nothing to the new order. Better that they be cleared out of the way, instead of inheriting anything."

Cyril was becoming more and more upset.

"There has always been rape and murder," he pointed out. "Would you not hesitate to encourage a rise in the committing of either of those?"

"But I am not talking about years. You forgot to mention the boundless joy that millions will feel when they learn they have a future."

"A future under the control of you and others of like mind? A future that was not in danger in the first place?"

"Yes, that, Cyril, every bit that. We can bring peace and prosperity throughout Europe. A healthy population is a happy one, and happy people buy goods, happy people buy land, happy people spend money that can filter down to the poor and raise them up as well."

Edling was looking pleased with himself, as though he were half-expecting some sort of medal to be bestowed upon him during the course of the banquet.

"And, naturally, they will look to you in gratitude," Cyril said. "Am I getting it right, Edling, or have I missed something?"

Someone tapped lightly on the door, hesitant about disturbing their privacy.

"Yes?" Edling asked imperiously.

"The banquet is about to begin. Everyone is waiting. You will be saying grace, will you not, sir?"

"I shall. We will be with you momentarily."

Edling took Cyril's hand.

"I plan to tell God how much I appreciate the protection with which He surrounded you so that you were able to return home safely at last," he said. "I plan to thank Him for *all* His blessings, past, present. . .and future. You will not let *everyone* down by causing a scene or going upstairs and pouting in your room, will you?"

Edling seemed unaccustomed to having his destiny firmly held in another man's hands.

"No, Harold, I will not embarrass you," Cyril told him resignedly. "I will not destroy what you plan, no matter how completely I disagree with you and how thoroughly repugnant I find the rules of the game you are playing."

For a moment, the prime minister's eyes seemed to be trying to pierce through into the center of his soul. Seconds passed, as though time had somehow frozen for the two of them.

Then Edling smiled broadly.

"Good! Now we should go."

"Harold?"

"Yes. . . ."

"What if the Muslims are wise enough to have figured all this out in advance?"

Edling hesitated and did not reply.

"What if they *have* a plan to spread the hantavirus throughout Europe?" Cyril added.

"Nonsense! My sources and yours for that matter would dispute any such notion. Besides, Cyril, the whole point is to seem ready, to be continually hatching plans for an offensive. If they were to start something, we would be in position to strike, however ironic that seems."

"Until much time had passed, and there was no indication of disease, and people bowed in gratitude before a merciful God."

"Your imagination is unbridled. Rein it in, my dear man. And do not burden others with such nonsensical speculation. In the end, God be the victor. Is that not what we believe as Christians?"

Cyril nodded obligatorily, and put on a smile that a more perceptive prime minister could have seen for what it was.

As he followed Edling out of that little room and into the bigger one, and they were slowly walking toward the banquet hall, the usual sycophants from the houses of Parliament and even the royal court at their very elbow, he thought that he could hear, for the briefest and most unwelcome moment, the distant cruel laughter of a strange little man standing in the funereal darkness of an underground tomb while gleefully rubbing together pale white hands not much bigger than a child's, the veins close to the surface, but then Lord Cyril Fothergill realized that this was only an inconvenient memory, not some new and disturbing reality, and he persuaded himself that he could ignore it at last, surely he could.